"David Massengill delivers near unbearable doses of suspense and shock in his post-apocalyptic chiller, *Red Swarm*. Deadly, flesh-seeking redbugs have taken over the Pacific Northwest, leaving behind a nightmare world for the survivors. Riveting, intense and unpredictable, *Red Swarm* takes the reader on a deliciously creepy, wild ride. With his masterfully macabre prose, Massengill does for bugs what Hitchcock did for our feathered friends in *The Birds*. You'll never be able to look at an insect the same way again. This is a must-read for horror fans!"

-Kevin O'Brien
No One Needs To Know
Tell Me You're Sorry

"Never have I read a novel that creeps me out so bad that I want to get it as far away from me as possible, like by tossing it onto a freighter headed overseas or something, and yet at the same time I find so compelling and insidious and engrossing and inevitable that I am forced to continue reading against my will, all the while feeling the phantom tingle of redbugs burrowing in my neck and turning me into a nest person. I hate you, David Massengill, for writing a book that is smart, witty, swiftly paced, and brilliantly conceived, yet at the same time is so creepy it makes my gums itch! Egad! I'm still having nightmares!"

-Garth Stein
A Sudden Light
The Art of Racing in the Rain

DAVID MASSENGILL is a Bay Area native who has lived in Seattle for nearly two decades. *Red Swarm* is his first novel. He is also the author of the short story collection *Fragments of a Journal Salvaged from a Charred House in Germany, 1816* (Hammer and Anvil Books). His short works of horror and literary fiction have appeared in numerous literary journals, including *Eclectica Magazine, Pulp Metal Magazine, Word Riot, The Literary Hatchet, The Raven Chronicles,* and *Yellow Mama,* among others. His stories have also appeared in the anthologies *Gothic Blue Book: The Revenge Edition, Gothic Blue Book IV: The Folklore Edition, State of Horror: California, Long Live the New Flesh: Year Two,* and *Clones, Fairies, & Monsters in the Closet.* Visit his website at www.davidmassengillfiction.com.

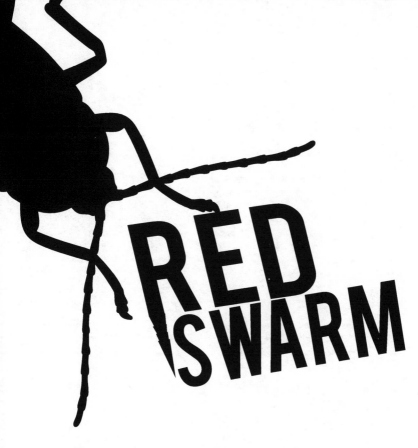

RED SWARM

MONTAG

Don,
Enjoy!

DAVID MASSENGILL

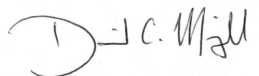

First Montag Press E-Book and Paperback Original Edition December 2015

Montag Press
ISBN: 978-1-940233-30-7
Cover art © 2015 Charlie Franco
Author photo © Stafford Lombard, Jr.
Cover, layout, & e-book © 2015 Blush Book Design

Montag Press Team:
Project Editor – Nicholas Morine
Managing Director – Charlie Franco

A Montag Press Book
www.montagpress.com
Montag Press
1066 47th Ave. Unit #9
Oakland CA 94601 USA

Montag Press, the burning book with the hatchet cover, the skewed word mark and the portrayal of the long-suffering fireman mascot are trademarks of Montag Press.

Printed & Digitally Originated in the United States of America
10 9 8 7 6 5 4 3 2 1

For my parents, Nancy and William

BOOK 1
DEBUGGING

From the second-to-last issue of *The Seattle Times:*

The Centers for Disease Control and Prevention estimates the death toll from the redbug infestation has passed the million mark.

Homeland Security has expanded the quarantine zone from western Montana, where the first fatalities occurred, to the Cascades in Washington state.

Although the CDC has confirmed the redbug kills a person by making physical contact and releasing a lethal toxin via its exoskeleton, the agency remains uncertain about the reason for the many "nest people" Homeland Security exterminators have been finding in the quarantine zone.

"We know the redbug burrows beneath this person's skin without killing its host," a CDC spokesperson announced at a press conference yesterday, "but we're not sure why. The entrance wound is almost always on the face or neck. Rather than die, many of the 'nest people' suffer a kind of dementia, drifting in and out of normal consciousness. The redbug seems to remain dormant under the skin of its host for an indefinite period of time. However, there have been cases where the redbug suddenly emerged from the nest person, and the insect was as deadly as ever."

"An orange VW camper van. Now that's something I didn't expect to see during the end of the world."

Carlos's eyes shot open when he heard Noah's voice from the front of the Humvee. Carlos sat up in the far back seat of the vehicle and glanced out the closed windows. Despite the air conditioning, the Humvee contained that metallic smell of insecticide and the potent scent of its passengers' sweat. Carlos realized that while he'd been sleeping his five-member extermination team had left the high desert and descended into a rust-colored canyon. The road paralleled a wide, slow-moving river, and parked near that river was the VW camper van.

The Humvee sped past it.

"Stop," Carlos called to Vince, who was driving.

"What'd you say?" Vince moved his bulbous, bald head to scowl at Carlos in the rearview mirror. He looked at Noah, who sat in the passenger seat, and said, "I think Sleeping Beauty has awoken to make a request."

Noah turned around in his seat and gave Carlos a friendly grin. "Buddy, we're heading to Mirror Lake for debugging."

"I thought we were going to Ephrata," Carlos said.

"We passed through while you were sleeping. We didn't bother spraying. There must have been a hell of a fire. The town looked like an ashtray."

Carlos unbuckled his seatbelt and stared out the rear window at the van, which was growing smaller in the distance. "Turn around, Vince," he said, his voice cracking. "I think that van belongs to someone I know."

"Well, I'm sure they're dead by now," Vince said. "Everyone in eastern Washington is dead."

"Aw, come on, Vince," Jared said. He sat next to his twin, Tyler, in the seat in front of Carlos. Twenty-two years old, the boyish-faced Jared and Tyler were the youngest members of the team. "Just let the man take a look."

"You're always slowing us down, Carlos," Vince said as he turned the Humvee around. "You know that? I wanted to get to Mirror Lake ASAP and radio camp. I haven't talked to the Director of Teams in a while."

Carlos didn't respond to his team leader, whose usually pale face had become an angry crimson in the rear view mirror. He only thought of his cousin Lucia and how the last time he'd seen her in Seattle she was hurrying to get back to an orange VW camper van.

"Okay, helmet's fastened," Carlos said as he stood alone outside the Humvee. He glanced down at his suit to check that he'd zipped it up all the way. The government had designed the clothing—a white weave of cotton, polybenzimidazole, and Kevlar—to be impervious to redbugs. But Carlos figured if the insects could creep inside the cupboards, closets, and drawers of homes he'd sprayed throughout eastern Washington, they could get inside his suit.

"Make it quick," Vince said, looking straight ahead in the direction of the road.

Carlos nodded, and then Jared closed the door from within the Humvee.

Carlos only heard his breath inside the helmet as he walked alone through tall, brown grass to reach the van. Sooty-looking clouds filled the September sky. The exterminator suits were surprisingly lightweight, but the muggy air made Carlos feel like he was encased in a hot, wet sponge. He only hoped he wouldn't have to run.

It had been six months since the redbugs had first appeared in Montana, and four months since they came to eastern Washington. All they had to do was land on your clothing or skin, and within 24 hours the poison on their legs and feelers ruined you. Rash, fever, seizures, skin necrosis, death.

But there had been survivors whom the redbugs never touched. Carlos's team had found some during this tour: a group of teenagers holed up in a gas station in Quincy and an ex-marine living in a motel on Interstate 90. Surely, more would appear.

Maybe even Lucia.

As he neared the van, Carlos recalled the day he'd last seen her. It was a little over a year ago, at the engagement party for her older brother, Hector, and his fiancée. Carlos spotted Lucia through a window as she came up the stairs to her parents' house in Seattle's Wedgwood neighborhood. He was glad he'd be able to talk to his eccentric cousin again. They hadn't spoken in months. He grinned when he saw she had a dyed blue streak and some blue feathers in her wavy, shoulder-length hair. She wore a suede fringe jacket over a turquoise dress that showed cleavage.

"OMG," Carlos's niece said, entering the living room. "Aunt Lucia just showed up with her lesbian lover. And get this: Her girlfriend drives an orange hippie bus."

Carlos now pressed his face against one of the side windows of the van. The glass was brown with grit, but he was still able to see the interior. In the back of the van was a table holding a few *Penthouse* magazines, a carton of American Spirit cigarettes, and torn-open packets of instant coffee. On the counter beyond the table were empty food cans. Carlos saw labels for refried beans, pork, clam chowder, cat food.

A horn honked.

Carlos glanced back at the Humvee. The vehicle's door was open again, and Jared was motioning for him to return. Carlos heard Jared calling out to him, but he couldn't discern the words.

Carlos held up his hand to signal for his team to wait. He needed to be sure this wasn't the van belonging to Azalea, Lucia's girlfriend.

He peered through the van's window again and saw a pile of men's crumpled clothing on the rearmost seat. Leaning against that pile was a shotgun. Carlos doubted Lucia would allow her girlfriend to have a rifle in her van. She'd declared early in life that she was a pacifist, and damn serious about it. He remembered when she'd squeezed his hand in back of the high school during his freshman year. His brother had just received his first medal in the Iran War, and Carlos was failing History. "Your parents may worship your brother," Lucia told her pouting cousin, "but how great is it to be a chemical soldier and carry around weapons that melt the skin off people? You, on the other hand, have a sense of compassion most males lack."

Carlos was certain this wasn't Azalea's van after he peered through the driver's-side window.

Sprawled across the front two seats was a man's corpse. The dead fellow wore a gray flannel shirt and soiled jeans. His head looked shrunken, and his lips were parted, as if he'd cried out while dying. He had the charred-looking skin and jaundiced eyes of all redbug victims. His keys were in the ignition.

The Humvee's horn sounded again, but this time it wasn't a honk. The sound was constant—and aggravating.

"The bastard," Carlos muttered, imagining Vince leaning against the horn with his bulky upper body. His team leader was always harping on him. *"Be more focused when we're debugging Main Street, Carlos." "You didn't spray long enough in that church basement, Carlos." "You can't snoop around apartments you're not assigned to, Carlos."*

Carlos forgot his irritation when he looked toward the Humvee again. Jared was wildly waving his arms at him. Both the twins pointed in the direction from which the Humvee had come. Jared pulled the door shut.

It was then that Carlos saw the redbugs spewing out of the rock wall down the road. They were forming a swarm. Carlos knew the protocol from the *Homeland Security Exterminator's Manual.* Seek shelter if an entire swarm is approaching. Although your suit protects you from the insects, a barrage by an entire swarm could crack your helmet right open.

Normally, Carlos would duck inside a building. But today he only had a choice between two vehicles, and one was too far away. The redbugs would probably reach him in a minute.

He yanked on the handle of the van's side door.

The door was locked.

"Damn." Carlos saw the swarm sweeping toward him like a massive dust cloud. Luckily, the driver's-side door creaked open.

Due to the rolled-up windows and the rotting body, noxious fumes greeted him inside the vehicle. Usually, Carlos's helmet diluted outside smells. But in here, he had to breathe through his mouth so he wouldn't vomit.

He slammed the door shut and frantically climbed over the dead man to reach the back of the van. He watched through the window as the swarm made a red haze around the Humvee. He squatted on the carpeted floor, knowing the insects would fly here next.

One redbug landed on the window closest to Carlos. He glanced up at the familiar, roach-like insect that clung to the glass with legs covered in tiny hairs. Its red, metallic-looking body was about the length of his middle finger. The redbug momentarily flapped its thin, brownish wings.

Soon there were four redbugs on the window.

Then seven.

Then dozens.

Even though Carlos knew he was safe inside the van, the insects still gave him goose bumps and a chill along his spine.

He lay on the floor so he'd have more distance from the redbugs, which continued to land on the window and block more and more light from outside. He'd found that if you remain still the redbugs sometimes lost interest in you.

Prone on the floor, he tried to assure himself he'd had good reasons for becoming an exterminator. He'd been fired from his job as a maintenance technician at a corporate office tower in Seattle. His boss had told him, "You can't perform well when you keep getting into these funks where you're zoning out on the job." Washington state's unemployment rate had risen to 21% after the 15-year Iran War ended about a year ago. His family had mentioned that Homeland exterminators made even more money than cops, and having a Homeland Security veteran in the Vasquez clan would be impressive.

His main reason, though, was that Lucia had stopped talking to him after the engagement party and moved to eastern Washington—the area of the state where redbugs were now decimating entire populations.

But he hadn't found Lucia after two month-long tours of duty, so what was the point of completing a third? He'd only see more decaying towns, more blackened corpses, more redbugs.

Weary of watching the insects search for a way inside the van and inside his suit, he turned his head away from the window and stared along the floor of the van. He saw under the rearmost seat what resembled a greeting card. He fished it out of the shadows with two fingers. On the cover of the card was a picture of a sun and moon above a pair of stick figures holding hands. Beneath the figures were the words:

THE SUN AND MOON FOLLOW YOU EVERYWHERE...

Carlos opened the card and read the rest of the words:

...BUT I'M ALWAYS BY YOUR SIDE

Happy 6-Month Anniversary, Lucia!

Yours Forever,
Azalea

Carlos was smiling at the card when the twins began calling to him from outside the van. The van that had truly belonged to Azalea. The van that had transported his cousin Lucia to eastern Washington. The van that had probably been stolen by the sorry corpse in the front seat. That bastard had eventually paid the price.

Carlos heard his team spraying the redbugs covering the van.

He raised himself from the floor and placed his face near the window. A blue foam now covered most of the glass and trapped writhing redbugs. Like all exterminators, he knew he was supposed to stay far away from the spray path of the insecticide—a highly carcinogenic combination of arsenic acid, lactofen, PCNB, and two experimental agents.

But Carlos didn't care about cancer right now. He was looking through a clear patch of glass at the expanse of desert soil. He wondered if his cousin had lived near here—and if she was living there still.

As the Humvee crept along Central Avenue, Carlos eyed the doorways and windows the vehicle passed. He noticed mom-and-pop shops resembling others he'd seen on past tours of eastern Washington: an antiques store with a grimy *Gone Fishin'* sign on its door, a real estate agency that had a quilt covering its broken front windows, a log-cabin hotel with a corpse draped over one of its balconies.

"Looks like Mirror Lake is as dead as all the rest of the towns," Vince said. He steered the Humvee into a parking lot bordering a small lake.

Carlos thought the greenish-blue body of water would have been beautiful if there wasn't a rusting semi-truck jutting out of its surface. The truck's trailer was lopsided from sinking into the muck at the bottom of the lake.

"You think you see your friend under that water?" Vince asked Carlos. He picked up his helmet from beside the driver's seat and placed it over his head. "You're welcome to swim out to the middle of the lake and take a look."

As usual, Carlos attempted to ignore his team leader. He felt guilty about dragging the other exterminators into a risky situation, but if he hadn't inspected that van he wouldn't know it was Azalea's. Before leaving the vehicle, he'd quickly checked the glove compartment and the dead man's pockets for something that would lead him to Lucia. The van provided no clue other than the card.

In preparation for his patrol, Carlos unfastened his extermination hose from the ceiling of the Humvee and checked his backpack for a first aid kit and his Meal, Ready-to-Eat. He then lied to his team. "I don't have grub. Would someone hand me another MRE?"

He recalled Lucia's dietary restrictions and said, "Make that a vegetarian MRE."

"You really need to watch yourself," Noah told Carlos as they ascended Central Avenue with their hoses pointed before them. Vince had assigned them this street. The twins were debugging Waterside Drive, and Vince was going to call the camp in Wenatchee and confirm the team should return by morning.

"Oh, yeah?" Carlos asked. "And why is that?" He tried to hide his annoyance. Though Noah was the teammate he liked the most, he disapproved of the man's need to always please people—especially Vince.

"Vince was talking about leaving you back at that van," Noah said.

Carlos stopped in the street and looked through the face shield of Noah's helmet. Noah stared back at him with those sky-blue, earnest eyes.

"I swear he was going to do it, buddy," Noah said. "After the swarm came. He said you'd jeopardized the safety of the team. I persuaded him not to."

Carlos glanced at the silver cross pinned to the front of Noah's uniform. He appreciated that Noah was able to hold onto his religion during these times. It seemed like hope had become a rarity for people.

"I'm starting to think Vince has it out for me," Carlos said, continuing along the road.

"He's not sure you're…tough enough to be on the team. I know you are. But Vince said he heard you crying in your sleep when we were in Quincy."

Carlos couldn't remember what dream had triggered the tears. He suffered from nightmares regularly. He recalled the one in which he, Lucia, and her brother Hector had stood in an intersection in the middle of a desert. Lucia argued with Hector while Carlos was between them. Hector wore the blue suit and tie he'd worn at his engagement party, and Lucia had on a crimson bathrobe. Hector informed Lucia she could only prove her point by opening her bathrobe. Carlos told his shame-faced cousin she didn't have to listen to her brother, but she opened the clothing anyway.

"You see?" Hector said in an accusing voice. He pointed at his sister, who had a redbug attached to each of her breasts.

Carlos now blinked a few times to get the bizarre dream out of his head. He comforted himself by thinking about the greeting card in the back of Azalea's van. He turned to Noah. "I was in a rough patch for a while," he said. "I'm feeling better about things now, though." He wanted to tell Noah about his search for Lucia, but he was concerned Noah would tell Vince. He didn't need Vince sabotaging his efforts.

"I guess we should start spraying," Noah said. They'd reached the block of Central Avenue where the businesses began. Noah motioned toward the yellow storefront of the Butter & Love Bakery. "I'll go in there."

Carlos looked across the street from the bakery and saw a post office with a smoke-stained doorway and a half-burnt American flag hanging out front. Next to the post office was what resembled a health foods store. On the cracked glass of the store's window were painted vegetables and the words *Enlightened Choices*. Carlos imagined Lucia and Azalea shopping there.

"I'll start with the health foods store," he said.

The door to Enlightened Choices was unlocked. The store was small, and a wide-open door in the rear kept the space from being completely dark. Carlos could see most of the shelves were empty. What remained were spiritual trinkets: incense holders, crystals, Buddha statues.

Carlos picked up one of the jade Buddhas and remembered Lucia telling him meditation was a way he could deal with his depression.

"Sit on the floor of your apartment the next time you get the blues," she'd said. "Don't try to shake off your sadness. Just focus on your breath for 5 minutes. The inhalations, the exhalations. You might find your depression starts to fade."

Of course, this talk occurred long before the engagement party. About a month after the party, Carlos's mom told him about Lucia moving away.

"She went with her...friend to some hippie community in eastern Washington," Carlos's mother had said.

"I've never thought of eastern Washington as being hippie-friendly," Carlos said. But then he thought of how his conservative family lived in Renton, which was just next to liberal Seattle.

Carlos's mother shrugged. "I suppose Lucia found the right town for her. She'll probably fit in there more than she fits in with her family. I'm glad you two have grown apart since you were teenagers. I don't think she's a good influence."

Moving toward the back of Enlightened Choices, Carlos passed the counter holding the cash register. The register drawer was open and empty. He thought he saw a dead man slumped against the wall behind the counter. He didn't peer too deeply into the shadows, however, because he didn't need to see yet another corpse. They had become as common as weeds.

What he did look at was the cluster of black specks on the patch of wall directly above the figure.

Those were redbug droppings.

Like roaches, redbugs fed on decaying organic matter and fermenting foods. Carlos noticed more droppings on the wall as he approached the back of the store. The feces were on and around a series of painted portraits of Native Americans. The spotted faces in the framed paintings stared stoically back at Carlos. Near the rear exit, the droppings became large smears, like black tar.

Carlos was about to begin spraying toward the front of Enlightened Choices when he noticed a hallway branching out of the rear left corner of the store. A sign indicated that restrooms were at the end of the hallway. To the left of that sign was the beginning of a bulletin board stretching into the darkness of the hallway.

Carlos wondered if the bulletin board might hold some clue that would lead him to Lucia's "hippie community." He started down the hallway with his hose lifted and ready to spray. He held his flashlight in his other hand, but he didn't want to turn it on just yet. Redbugs were even more attracted to light than they were to movement or noise.

He heard a wet, suctioning sound beneath his boots, and he wondered if one of the restrooms was leaking water.

Then he thought of blood. He remembered with a shudder that Lake Chelan cottage he'd entered on his last tour. A young husband and wife had slit their wrists together and died sitting up in bed. The mattress and the rug beneath the bed were crusted with blood.

The sucking sound grew louder, and Carlos felt his boots sticking to the floor. He figured he'd probably reached the middle of the hallway. He clicked on his flashlight and looked at the floor.

It was covered in a network of redbug nests.

He lifted one boot from the orange, gelatinous substance that formed the hundreds of toe-like egg sacs. Each sac encased brown, pill-shaped eggs. The flashlight in Carlos's trembling hand shone on his leg.

Redbugs speckled his thigh.

And his waist.

And his arms.

Carlos cried out as he brushed the bugs off his suit. During his movements, the flashlight shone on the walls and ceiling of the hallway, revealing that the nests covered the entire area—including the bulletin board.

He was only able to see a portion of a flyer on the bulletin board. The piece of paper announced *–seeking naturopaths to help us find immunity from the bug-*

"Carlos!"

The voice was Noah's, and it came from the front of the store.

Carlos sprayed the hallway as he walked backwards along the way he'd come. He glanced toward the front of the store and saw Noah's head peeking inside the door.

"Hurry up, buddy," Noah said. "I've got something to show you."

Carlos continued spraying as he made his way to the entrance. The insecticide's blue foam soon lined the shelves and filled the cash register and concealed the spiritual trinkets. One of the Buddhas fell to the floor and shattered. Carlos saw a few redbugs escape the hallway and fly outside the rear door.

He heard the front door open behind him. When he stopped spraying, he turned and saw Noah standing in the doorway. Waiting on the sunlit sidewalk beyond him was a small, sixty-something woman with thin, cloud-like hair dyed an orangeish-brown. She wore a green dress patterned with tiny yellow flowers.

"This is Helena," Noah said. "She works in the bakery."

"Why didn't you cover her?" Carlos asked. After stepping outside Enlightened Choices, he unzipped his backpack to search for a Hazard Wrap—the plastic, redbug-proof poncho exterminators draped over survivors they found in the field. The wraps included face shields and gloves and were more lightweight than exterminator uniforms.

Noah touched Carlos's arm, indicating he should stop looking for the wrap. He said, "I'm pretty sure she's one of...."

Carlos zipped up his backpack and stared at Helena. She smiled at both exterminators.

"I must get back to my cakes," she said in a slightly monotone voice. "Today's the first day of fall, so I'm making an apple cake."

Carlos glanced at Noah and whispered, "Where's the wound?"

"Back of the neck," Noah mumbled, and then he returned to grinning at Helena.

Carlos had never seen any nest people before. He'd heard exterminators were finding a lot of them in the quarantine zone's largest cities—Billings, Missoula, Boise, Spokane. Carlos's tours had mostly been confined to small towns. Vince had recently debriefed the team on nest people. He said they usually remain in dazed states, and they're unaware of the insects living under their skin. All of them have entrance wounds on the face or neck. The insect enters with a sharp, barbed appendage that emerges from beneath its chin, slices open the skin, and helps pull the redbug inside. The appendage secretes a numbing substance that prevents a person from feeling much pain.

When the redbug exits the body, the nest person dies.

"We should do the check," Noah said. "Like Vince taught us."

Carlos watched the kind-faced woman. She continually glanced over her shoulder at the bakery.

"I must get back to my cakes," she began again.

"Can we at least take her inside somewhere?" Carlos asked. "Just in case she's not really...."

Noah nodded. "But not in the bakery. I found egg sacs all over the kitchen counters." He looked at Helena. "We'll let you get to your cakes soon enough." He spoke loudly, as if he were addressing a partially deaf person. "Maybe we can even taste your apple cake."

"Will you please lift your hair so I can look at the back of your neck?" Carlos said. He stood behind Helena, who sat in a chair in the middle of the Cascades Bank lobby. All the other chairs were tipped over, and papers and brochures lay scattered across the bank's desks. Carlos looked outside one of the front windows and saw Noah spray painting a mark on the glass door of the Butter & Love Bakery.

An *X* meant Homeland Security exterminators had sprayed a bug-infested space. An *O* meant the space had been bug-free but the exterminators sprayed anyway.

Noah completed his *X* and then started across the street to mark the health foods store Carlos had debugged.

Carlos figured he only had a few minutes to be alone with Helena. "Do you know a woman named Lucia Vasquez?" he asked.

Helena lifted her hair as Carlos had instructed. Her neck showed the scabbed-over slit where the redbug had burrowed inside her. The scab looked fresh. Carlos figured the insect had entered her only a few days ago.

"I think Lucia lives around here somewhere," he said. "She's 29—the same age as me. She has long, dark-brown hair with maybe a blue streak in it. Her eyes and nose look like mine." He stepped to Helena's side so she could peer up at his facial features through his helmet.

"We'll be selling pumpkin cake in a couple weeks," she said in a pensive voice. "And soon enough all the Thanksgiving pies."

"So you don't know Lucia," Carlos said, trying not to be irritated by the woman's useless response. After all, Helena only had half a mind—if that.

He began palpating the skin of her neck as Vince had shown the team. The redbug can get deep enough beneath the skin to be invisible, Vince had said. But you should always be able to feel it.

Carlos didn't feel anything. He wondered if he should try a facial exam.

"You said Lucia would like to buy a Thanksgiving pie?" Helena asked. "We'll have chocolate pecan this year."

"I asked if you know Lucia. She's often with a woman named Azalea. I've never met-"

"Azalea," Helena said, suddenly beaming. "Such a pretty name. Such a pretty girl. She likes my red velvet cupcakes."

"You know Azalea!" Carlos erupted.

"I always listen when people praise my baking." Helena pointed at her left ear. "You've got to listen to things like that," she said.

Carlos noticed the skin behind that ear was red and swollen. He kneeled to more closely inspect the area.

He saw the swelling was in the shape of an insect.

"Where does Azalea live?" he asked.

Helena paused and then said, "Such a pretty name. Such a pretty girl."

"Does she live near here?" Carlos pressed her while gently probing the woman's reddened skin with his index finger. The redbug immediately shifted beneath the flesh, and Helena gave a brief, high-pitched cry.

"I'm sorry," Carlos said. "Did I hurt you?"

"I must get back to my cakes," Helena said, sounding distraught. "Today's the first day of fall, so I'm making an apple cake."

Carlos was about to ask about Azalea again when the door to the bank opened and Noah entered.

"Did you find it?" Noah asked.

"You can let your hair down now," Carlos told Helena. He stood and looked at Noah. "She's one of them," he said.

Noah nodded. "Did she tell you anything we didn't already know?"

"Not really." Carlos watched Helena to see if she'd reveal his lie.

She turned around in her chair to look at the men and said, "And soon enough all the Thanksgiving pies."

Carlos watched Noah place an arm around Helena as they led her in the direction of the Humvee.

Noah grinned at the woman. He told her, "You know, you remind me of my grandmother."

Helena was silent. She'd developed a pained look on her face when they started walking away from the bakery.

"Are either of your grandmothers still alive?" Noah asked Carlos.

Carlos shook his head. He remembered his Grandma Milena, a cheerful, heavyset woman who folded you in flesh whenever she hugged you. She'd watched over Carlos and all his cousins when they were children. She'd often keep Lucia and him inside her little yellow house with her while the others ran about the backyard with their slingshots or their water guns.

"You two are the sensitive ones," she'd once said while serving them her famous Christmas Eve tamales. "*Los sensibles.* You feel much for others, but others won't always feel much for you. What's important is that you watch out for each other."

Carlos sighed to himself and told Noah, "All my grandparents are dead."

"Well, Helena is going to be just fine," Noah said, using his loud voice again. He squeezed the woman's shoulder. "We're going to get you to a refugee center in Seattle. The doctors there will help you get back to your normal self."

Carlos thought how Noah was providing false hope. He'd heard it was impossible to restore the mental capacity of a nest person.

"I'll need more powder sugar for the icing," Helena muttered in a concerned voice.

"We'll find you some," Noah said. He kept his arm around her as they crossed the street toward Vince.

The team leader stood beside the Humvee, scowling at the green radio in his hand. He pressed a button and held the radio against his ear. He watched the approaching trio with bleary eyes.

"I haven't been able to get through to camp," he said. "I keep trying, but there's only static. I'm hoping the Director of Teams will radio me." He removed the radio from his ear and looked at Helena. "Who's this?"

"Found her in a bakery," Noah said. "Her name's Helena."

"A survivor." Vince sounded impressed.

"She's got a wound on the back of her neck," Carlos said. He tried to make eye contact with his team leader, but Vince's eyes barely met his. Carlos could tell Vince was still angry with him about the van incident.

"She's got one of those injuries you told the team about," Carlos added.

"She's a nest person?" Vince asked, looking at Noah.

Carlos could tell Noah was trying to figure out how to respond without upsetting Helena. Carlos questioned whether the woman was even capable of comprehending her situation.

"I was going to have her wait in the Humvee," Noah said. "I can sit with her. I'm guessing we should take her to the camp as soon as possible."

"I told you I haven't been able to reach anyone," Vince said, shaking his head in annoyance, "so I'm not going to have a damn nest person hanging out in my vehicle all day." He looked down at the radio. "Take her inside one of the houses around here. The twins finished debugging most of this street. I'll honk the horn when I'm ready for you."

"Where are the twins now?" Carlos asked.

"I told them to take a break so they'd stay out of my hair," Vince said, pressing the radio against his ear again.

Carlos considered mentioning that Vince had no hair. Instead, he said, "I'd like to take a break, too."

He saw Noah shoot him a warning look, but he ignored it. A break would give him a better sense of the town's layout, and knowing the town would only help him in his search for Lucia.

"I can be back in 15," he told Vince.

"You're really pushing it, Carlos," Vince growled.

Noah grabbed Carlos's arm and pulled him in the direction of the houses across the street.

Though intimidated, Carlos managed not to look away from Vince's glare. "I'll take my break later then," he told his team leader.

Carlos kept seeing red *X*'s sprayed on the stairs and paths leading to the houses of Waterside Drive. He guessed this street included some of the most desirable real estate in town. Many of the houses were three-stories tall and had sizeable front yards. Some offered porches, and a few even had upstairs balconies overlooking the lake.

Of course, all the homes reflected the current state of eastern Washington. Gardens were brown and shriveled. Wooden boards concealed windows. Garbage cans and their former contents blocked driveways. A row of five dark and withered corpses lined a yellow lawn.

"There's an *O*!" Noah said. "We can go in there." He pointed at a white, peak-roofed house that was a couple blocks from the Humvee. Carlos glanced back at Vince and thought he saw him speaking into the radio. He considered how Vince had never had difficulty reaching the camp before.

"I think I want to lie down in a real bed," Noah said. He started up the stone path leading to the house's porch. He held Helena's hand, and she slowly trailed behind him. Noah turned to look at Carlos and asked, "Is it all right with you if I nap for 10 minutes?"

Carlos and Noah had often complained to each other about having to sleep on floors with their team. Vince never allowed the exterminators to be far from one another at night, and that usually meant their sleeping quarters were warehouses or corporate offices.

"You can nap," Carlos said, "but after you wake up you've got to let me take a 10-minute walk around town. And you can't tell Vince."

"Do I look like a snitch?" Noah asked.

Rather than respond, Carlos eyed the mosquito netting stretching between all the porch's pillars. The netting had obviously failed to keep redbugs away from the house. Tears showed throughout the fabric.

Carlos stopped and peered into the shadows of the porch to look for redbugs.

Noah motioned for him to continue up the porch's stairs and through the largest hole in the netting. "Come on," he said. "The twins wouldn't have sprayed an *O* if there were bugs inside."

Carlos followed behind Helena. He noticed she was tugging absently on her earlobe.

Noah pushed the front door open, and they entered a narrow hallway with hardwood floors and a blue-carpeted stairway leading to the second floor. To the left was a living room and to the right a dining room. Both chambers were traditionally furnished and pleasantly lit by late-afternoon sunlight coming through windows.

Noah walked into the living room and set his extermination hose on a chair. He fell back onto a plush, aqua-green sofa and folded his arms over his chest as if he were hugging himself. He looked strange lounging on the sofa in his exterminator helmet and uniform.

"This is the kind of house we both deserve after we kill all the bugs and the world is a peaceful place again," he said.

Carlos joined him in the living room and sat on a leather recliner. He set his hose on the blue-and-green striped rug. Despite its tranquility, the house unnerved him. It reminded him of Lucia and Hector's parents' house and that unfortunate evening of the engagement party. He remembered hearing the DING-DANG-DONG sound of their doorbell while Lucia had stood just outside the front door.

"Wouldn't you want to live in a house like this?" Noah asked.

"I'm fine with my apartment in Seattle," Carlos said. He pictured his one-bedroom home, which was in Seattle's Columbia City neighborhood. He'd lived there since his early twenties. The apartment didn't have a view or a deck, but Carlos appreciated the huge, familiar cedar tree that brushed against the living room window on windy days, and the skylight in the bedroom. When his depression was weighing on him or he was obsessing about what his brother's death in Iran must have been like, Carlos would lie on his bed and stare through that skylight, watching clouds form and pass and eventually give way to stars. Seeing the stars gave him perspective.

"Wait until you find yourself a wife," Noah said. "She'll make you want a house. That's how it was with Katie and me. She pointed out that a family wouldn't be able to fit inside our rented townhouse in Ravenna."

"Sometimes a family won't fit inside anywhere," Carlos said. He recalled how when Lucia had come through that front door at the engagement party all the Vasquezes seemed to freeze. Then Hector stomped toward her in his shiny black shoes.

"Helena?" Noah asked, shooting the nest person a worried look. She remained in the hallway, frowning and rubbing her ear. She looked from the living room to the dining room as if she were seeking a place to hide.

Noah consoled her, "The people at the refugee center in Seattle are going to help you feel better."

"I told you I wanted to get back to my cakes," Helena said in a resentful voice. She shuffled into the dining room and stood in one corner. Facing the wall, she continued to fuss with her ear.

Noah looked at Carlos and shrugged. "You said you recently broke up with your girlfriend?" he asked.

Carlos nodded. "We realized we had nothing in common."

He recalled the way Ana had shaken her head at the engagement party. "You'd think your cousin would have enough sense not to come here," she said. "She knows the family doesn't approve of the lesbian thing."

Carlos almost told Ana she shouldn't act like she was one of the family when they'd only been dating for six months. But he didn't say that because the truth was Ana meshed with his family better than he did. His sister had introduced him to Ana after befriending her in a Zumba class. Carlos's mother had informed him, "We'd be proud to call Ana your girlfriend."

"This job can be tough on a relationship," Noah said. He fingered the cross on his uniform and gazed outside the window, where the sky was growing dim with the approaching evening. "You see things people shouldn't see."

Carlos had never seen those things while he was dating Ana. They'd split up before his first tour of duty. He'd just lost his position as a maintenance technician when Ana barged into his apartment and told him, "It's hard enough being with someone who's depressed all the time and never tells me what's wrong. And now you have no job. It's a shame this isn't going to work.

I think your family and I were kind of falling in love with each other."

Noah asked Carlos, "You still with me, buddy? Are you thinking about one of those things you shouldn't have seen?"

Actually, Carlos was thinking about Lucia again, and how he would have liked to talk with her after his break-up with Ana. He was sure his cousin would have had some perceptive comment about his dating a 22-year-old who worked at a soap store.

"Weren't you going to take that nap?" he asked Noah. He decided he would get back to asking Helena about Azalea while Noah slept.

"Wake me in 20?" Noah asked. He rose from the sofa and walked to the bottom of the stairs. "I'll take care of our friend when you do your exploring."

Carlos glanced at Helena, who still stood in the corner of the dining room. She now rested her head against the wall. She'd finally stopped touching her ear.

"Carlos!" Noah called from upstairs in a loud whisper.

Carlos guessed Noah had found redbugs in the house. He jumped up from his chair and retrieved his extermination hose from the rug. He saw Helena had beaten him to the staircase. She mounted the stairs, her hand on her ear once again.

"Sugar," she mumbled. "Flour, butter...."

"Watch out, Helena," Carlos said, pushing past her on the staircase. He found Noah at the top of the stairs. Hanging on the wall behind him was a framed photo of an elderly couple with smiling faces. The man and woman wore Hawaiian leis around their necks, and they stood barefoot on a black sand beach. A reddish-orange sunset lit up the horizon.

Noah motioned with his hand toward a closed door next to the landing. Carlos heard through that door what sounded like someone taking a shower.

"We're not alone," Noah said. He went to the door and turned its handle.

"I'll go first," Carlos said. He glanced behind him and saw that Helena had reached the landing. He entered the room with his hose pointed before him.

He found a bedroom in disarray. The mirrored closet door was open, as were the drawers of two dressers. Suits, sweaters, and men's and women's shoes lay scattered on the floor and bed. It looked as if the house's owners had packed in a hurry.

Near the bed was another closed door. The sound of the running water continued inside.

"Hello?" Carlos spoke through the door. He glanced back at Noah, who'd entered the bedroom. Helena stood just behind him, blinking her eyes rapidly.

The door swung open and the shower stopped.

Tyler stood inside the bathroom. He wore his exterminator suit but no helmet. Shaving cream covered half his face, and he held a razor in one hand.

"Hey, guys," he said. "Did Vince send you after us? Jared and I decided to get cleaned up. Who's that?" He pointed the razor at Helena.

Carlos remembered Vince's warning about nest people: Stay suited up whenever you're around them.

"Put your helmet on," Carlos told Tyler. He felt a sudden dread. He glanced back at Helena, who had begun moaning. She cupped her hand over her ear.

"Helmet on now!" he shouted. When he looked at the bathroom again he saw Jared standing next to his brother. Jared was naked except for a purple towel around his waist.

"She's a nest person," Noah said to the twins in a panicked voice.

Carlos quickly stepped toward the bathroom and slammed the door shut. "Get dressed," he spoke through the door. And then he told Noah, "Take her downstairs."

As he watched Noah steer Helena toward the landing he spotted the red, wet wound behind her ear. A redbug crawled across the back of her neck and took flight.

Carlos immediately sprayed in the direction of the bug. The insecticide's blue foam clung to the ceiling above the bed and knocked over a small lamp on a nightstand.

The redbug, however, landed on the floor by the bathroom and scurried through the crack beneath the door.

Carlos figured the twins may have had time to fully cover themselves inside the bathroom.

But then he saw the suit and helmet resting on a chair in one corner of the room.

"Jared!" he called.

He yanked open the bathroom door and was relieved to find Tyler with helmet on. Tyler was shaking his head, and his eyes filled with tears as he looked in the direction of the shower.

Carlos saw Jared through the wet glass of the closed shower door. He lay trembling in the bathtub with the towel concealing most of his legs and torso.

Carlos noticed the smashed bug on the wall above the tub. The yellow goo of its innards was smeared across one tile.

It was also smeared across the palm of Jared's right hand.

Jared held that hand up for Carlos to see. His eyes were tearing in the same way as his brother's. "It landed on my neck," he whimpered. "Does this mean I'm going to die?"

Carlos watched Tyler help his brother along the stone path leading from house to sidewalk. Tyler was trying to move quickly, but Jared was hobbling. Night had fallen, and Carlos held his flashlight so the twins could see where they walked. The flashlight occasionally illuminated the solemn expressions past the face shields of their helmets.

Rashes had already formed on Jared's cheeks. Carlos guessed he'd live until tomorrow if he were lucky.

"Do you see Vince?" Noah asked Carlos. He shadowed the twins with his arm around Helena's waist. Helena moved stiffly and her face glistened with sweat, but she showed no fear of her impending death.

"I can't see him or the Humvee," Carlos said, pointing his flashlight in the direction of where Vince had parked the vehicle.

"Don't jerk your light around like that," Tyler snapped. "We don't want to attract a swarm or something."

Carlos continued to look for Vince and the vehicle, but he only saw silhouettes of houses and trees lining Waterside Drive.

The Humvee's headlights blinked on and shone green-yellow, like some creature's eyes peering out at them from the darkness. The headlights soon went out, and Carlos found himself dreading the meeting with their team leader.

Nearing the Humvee, he saw Vince leaning against the front bumper with his arms folded over his chest. Carlos lifted his flashlight so he could see Vince's face inside the helmet. He spotted a furrowed brow and glaring eyes.

"Get that light out of my face," Vince said, moving into a standing position. "I don't believe I honked the horn for you guys to come."

"It's Jared," Tyler said, his voice revealing his anxiety. He brought his brother before the team leader. "A bug landed on his skin." Tyler explained how the redbug had come from Helena and found its way inside the bathroom.

Vince frowned at Carlos and asked, "You brought that nest person around the twins when they weren't suited up?"

Noah stepped forward. "Carlos and I didn't know-"

"I wasn't talking to you," Vince said. He clicked on his own flashlight and shone it inside Jared's helmet. "How you doing, buddy?" he asked. The irritation in his voice was stronger than the sympathy.

Jared muttered something incomprehensible.

"I'm sorry," Carlos said. "We thought we were alone in that house."

Vince shook his head in disapproval. He told Tyler, "Get Jared inside the Humvee now. You'll find some C-99 syringes in the glove compartment. Give him a shot in the neck."

Carlos watched Tyler usher his brother toward one of the rear doors of the vehicle. Carlos had never known an exterminator who'd had to receive C-99. Homeland Security gave supplies of the experimental drug to its extermination teams a couple months ago. The drug didn't prevent your death if you came into contact with redbug toxin, but researchers claimed it could increase your lifespan by a week or more. Only a few of the drug's side effects were known.

The door shut, and Vince looked at Carlos again. He aimed his flashlight at Carlos's eyes. "I think your decisions are harming the team," he said.

"Vince," Noah said, "this wasn't his fault. I-"

"Shut up," Vince barked, "before I start in on you, too."

Carlos felt the familiar anger toward Vince rising up in him, but he tried to suppress it. After all, there was truth to Vince's words. He had been the one to lead Noah and Helena inside the bedroom.

But Vince wasn't aware of that.

Carlos knew challenging his team leader right now might cause him to lose his job, and how would he be able to find Lucia if he were no longer an exterminator?

"You're right," he told Vince. "We should have made sure the house was completely clear before going inside."

"'Should,'" Vince said, shaking his head and sneering. "I know that word. I should never have let you watch over a nest person when you can barely focus on your job as an exterminator. I should never have tolerated you slowing down our team by checking out that goddamn van. I should have dropped you off at the camp after I found those anti-depressants in your duffle bag in Quincy."

"What?" Carlos asked. He thought of the little orange bottle of pills he always kept rolled up in a sock at the bottom of his bag. He was annoyed by Vince's snooping, but he was also concerned about Homeland Security possibly asking him about his "NO" response to the application question *Do you have a history of depression?*

"Oh, yes," Vince said. "I know about your mental health problems. And you should know that mental health concerns are a reason for a team leader to terminate an exterminator."

"Vince," Noah said, "I've done a lot of debugging with Carlos, and I-"

"You'll be quiet for the last time," Vince said, holding up his hand to silence Noah.

Vince brought the flashlight closer to Carlos's eyes, making him squint. Carlos thought he might have swung at his team leader if Vince wasn't wearing a helmet.

"I'd drive you back to camp now if we had a camp to go to," Vince told Carlos, "but we don't."

Carlos's eyes went wide. He and Noah exchanged surprised looks.

"That's right, gentlemen," Vince said. He stopped pointing the flashlight at Carlos's face. He glanced at the Humvee before lowering his voice. "The Director of Teams finally radioed me. They had to break up camp and route all the other teams back to Seattle. The redbugs are now in western Washington."

"I've got to reach Katie," Noah said. "She-"

"You're not the only one with a wife," Vince said.

Carlos thought of his family. Though he worried about his parents, he knew his brother Benny would get them to a safe place. He also thought of the extended Vasquez clan, but none of them occupied his heart the way Lucia did. He wondered what would happen to Hector. His cousin patrolled downtown Seattle as a cop.

"Why didn't they call our team back to Seattle?" Noah asked.

"They tried," Vince said. "But they couldn't get through, and they had to leave. I figure they tried to reach us while we were all wasting time at that van. Carlos was the one who insisted we stop."

Carlos knew Vince was just continuing his usual harassment, but he couldn't help but feel guilty. He glanced at Noah, and he noticed his friend avoid eye contact.

"Well, we should start the drive to Seattle," Noah said. "We can be there in about three hours."

"Not enough gas for that," Vince said. "The Director told me we need to hunker down in Mirror Lake until we receive further word."

"We can go back to that house," Carlos said. "It's free of nests, and there's room enough for all of us." He turned his light on Helena, who stood a few feet behind Noah. Her sweating face had soaked the collar of her dress, and she stared ahead of her with glassy eyes. Carlos spotted a couple redbugs resting on one of her cheeks.

"She's not going anywhere with us," Vince said. "Thanks to her, one of my men is going to die."

"Vince!" Tyler called from the Humvee. He'd cracked open the rear door. "Jared's having a seizure."

"Move that woman farther away from the vehicle," Vince told Noah. "She's crawling with bugs." Before entering the Humvee, he scanned his suit with the flashlight to check for insects.

Noah led Helena from the parking lot onto the gravel of the beach. Carlos followed. He heard Jared's moaning coming from the Humvee.

"I wish you would have listened to me," Noah said. "I knew we shouldn't have checked out that van."

Carlos didn't respond. He turned off his flashlight and stared out at the black water with a frown on his face.

"Katie's not going to know what to do," Noah said. "We've got the basement, and we've got Hazard Wraps and food and water down there. But she depends on me for a lot."

"I'm sorry," Carlos said in a shaky voice. Despite the darkness, he could see Noah touching his cross again.

"I know everyone's got a theory for the redbugs," Noah said. "The radiation leak from that plant in Montana, and the chemical soldiers accidentally bringing them back from Iran.… But I keep thinking this is some kind of punishment from above."

Carlos remained silent. He remembered sitting in a sunlit park with Lucia after one particularly horrendous spell of depression he'd had during his early twenties. She'd told him, "I've sometimes thought that if we never have bad things happen to us we'll never grow."

"Noah, I need you," Vince called from the Humvee.

Once Noah entered the vehicle, Carlos walked over to a rear passenger window. The Humvee's ceiling lights showed Jared lying on the far back seat, where Carlos had napped earlier in the day. Jared no longer wore his helmet. Tyler sat by his feet, holding his ankles so he wouldn't move so much during his seizure. Noah pressed his shoulders against the seat, and Vince directed a syringe into his neck.

Jared's body jerked violently, and then he was still.

Carlos knocked on the window, causing his teammates to look up at him.

He heard Vince's muted voice: "Don't open that door. I don't want any bugs in here."

"Can I help?" Carlos shouted.

Vince shook his head. After giving Jared the shot, he moved to the front of the vehicle. He picked up the receiver for the megaphone system.

His voice soon boomed out of the speaker on top of the Humvee: "Finish off the nest person."

"'Finish off?'" Carlos asked, his eyes growing large. "You want me to-?" He glanced at Helena's shadowy figure. She still stood on the beach.

"She's a goner anyway," Vince said. "You'll be putting her out of her misery, and we won't have to deal with her anymore."

Horrified, Carlos thought how Jared was a "goner," too. He told Vince, "I won't kill her."

"Then take her back to where you found her. I'm sick of you standing around arguing with me. Don't return here. I can find you with the tracker chip in your suit. I'll get you when I'm ready to."

Carlos peered into the rear of the vehicle again and saw none of his teammates looked at him. Their eyes were on Jared. He recalled one fight he'd had with his father when he was in high school. During a family dinner, his father told him to stop moping and to "try mattering to the world like your brother mattered."

None of his other family members looked at him after his father made the comment.

Carlos fetched his extermination hose from where he'd propped it against the Humvee. He retrieved Helena from the beach, and they headed into the darkness of the town.

As he wandered through Mirror Lake, Carlos decided to rely on moonlight rather than his flashlight. He didn't want to wear out the battery. He also didn't want to see more of what the flashlight had shown him: burnt shells of cars, the husks of redbug nests dangling from dead trees, a skeleton sprawled beneath a bus stop bench.

He thought how his team probably wouldn't care much if he died in town, but the idea affected him less when he imagined finding Lucia.

After all, she was what mattered most.

He remembered when he'd wandered away from that Vasquez reunion picnic in Moses Lake at the age of 16. He'd found a bridge over train tracks, and he sat on the railing of that bridge while he listened for the sound of the next train. He figured if he could go through with it he'd experience great pain for only a few seconds, and then all would be blackness. When the train appeared from behind a hillside, he felt someone's arms around his middle, holding him tightly.

"You don't have to be anyone you're not," Lucia had said. "You don't have to be your brother now that he's gone. You don't have to be the person your family wants you to be. I love you as you are. And I'm not the only one who will love you as you are."

Carlos shook off his reverie when he heard that ominous, low-pitched humming sound of a redbug swarm. The swarm sounded close.

Carlos hoped to find bug-free shelter where he could open his MRE. He hadn't eaten since morning, and low blood sugar was muddling his mind. If he could eat, he could gain some mental clarity about what to do with Helena. He wasn't comfortable just leaving her at the bakery—even if she was going to die soon.

"How are you, Helena?" he asked. He looked behind him, where she dragged herself through an intersection. Her breathing had become a wheezing, and she began to cough.

"We'll have a rest soon," he said, guessing she wouldn't be able to walk for much longer. He considered trying to talk to her about Azalea again, but he doubted she would speak. She hadn't offered a single word since they'd left the team at the vehicle.

On the corner ahead of him was a brick building supporting a large sign reading *LAKESIDE GYM*. Carlos figured a gym would be a less than desirable nesting place for redbugs. The insects seemed to prefer locations where there was organic decay, like grocery stores, restaurants, and people's homes.

He clicked on his flashlight and pointed it at the windows. None of the glass was broken or even cracked. When Carlos shone the light through one window, he saw exercise mats on the floor and racks of free weights lining a mirrored wall.

"Let's try to get in there," he told Helena.

Surprisingly, the entrance was unlocked. Carlos motioned for Helena to follow him inside, and then he carefully shut the door. He walked past the gym's front desk and eyed the large, one-room workout space for signs of redbugs. His flashlight revealed the walls and corners were clear of the insects and their droppings.

He noticed a door on the left side of the mirrored wall. He tried opening it, but it wouldn't budge. On another wall were entrances to the locker rooms. A tipped-over garbage can and a pile of towels blocked the doorway of the men's locker room.

Carlos sat on a weight bench and searched through his backpack for his MRE. "Want something to eat?" he asked Helena. He decided he could share his meal with her. He was saving the vegetarian MRE in case he found Lucia.

Helena didn't respond. She remained by the front door, staring out at the night.

Carlos lifted his face shield just enough to allow him to eat. He knew he probably should have checked the locker rooms before exposing his skin, but he figured he was already vulnerable. If Vince decided to abandon him here, he'd only last so long with his current food and insecticide supplies. And Carlos now doubted the team would come for him. He'd probably pissed Vince off too many times.

He heard a creaking sound while he forked cold beef ravioli into his mouth. The sound came from behind the locked door.

"Hello?" he asked, setting his meal on the bench.

He lowered his face shield and picked up his extermination hose. He went to the door and pressed his ear against its surface.

He didn't hear anything.

Then Helena began to whimper.

Carlos turned toward her and saw she'd opened the front door all the way. She stood in the center of the doorway.

"What are you doing?" Carlos said. "You're going to let in-"

Helena cut him off with a shriek. She screamed continuously as the swarm of redbugs filled the room.

Carlos shrank into the corner of the room and watched Helena vanish inside a cloud of redbugs. The flashlight fell out of his hand and rolled under a rack of barbells.

He didn't bother spraying because his hose would never be able to kill this many insects. Instead, he turned toward the locked door to protect his face shield.

The door suddenly pushed against him, and Carlos saw someone in a black nylon face mask peek out at him.

"Get in here!" The voice belonged to a woman.

Once inside the room, Carlos saw it was candlelit. He guessed he'd entered some kind of dance studio when he saw a railing spanning the length of another mirrored wall.

Three rows of five white body bags lined the studio floor. Blue, sweet-scented candles burned near the heads of two of the figures. Rings of daisies encircled the candles.

Carlos looked at the person standing beside him. In addition to her mask, she wore a black bodysuit. Carlos was stunned. Few of the survivors he'd encountered on his tours were equipped against redbugs. Usually, they were half-dead.

"My name's Rachel," she said.

"Carlos." He considered shaking her hand, but he thought they would barely feel each other through the material that covered their entire bodies.

"I'm sorry I couldn't bring your friend in here," she said. "The bugs would have gotten inside."

Carlos nodded. "That wasn't the first time she's come in contact with redbugs. She's a nest person. I don't think they can hurt her more than they already have."

"We'll go out there after the swarm leaves." Rachel went to the figures with the candles by their heads. She kneeled and looked down at the body bags.

"Who are these people?" Carlos asked.

"These two were my parents," Rachel said, indicating the body bags closest to her. "The rest were townspeople. They've been here for more than a month. My brother and some other men carried them in here."

"Where's your brother now?"

"Daniel went to get my youngest sister from her summer camp in Idaho. Then he's bringing her back here."

Carlos almost told her everyone in Idaho was dead and the government was considering bombing some cities in that state, but he didn't want to ruin her fantasy, nor did he know her well enough to know how she might react to such news. And besides, there probably were some survivors in Idaho. His team had found survivors in eastern Washington. He might find Lucia.

"Are you alone?" he asked.

Rachel didn't respond. After a pause, she asked, "And what are you doing here?"

Carlos told her he was an exterminator with Homeland Security, and he shared a bit about the day's events. He didn't mention he was possibly stranded in Mirror Lake.

"Would you like to get out of this town?" he asked. "My team might be able to take you to Seattle. There are redbugs in the city now, but there are also refugee centers. They're supposed to be insect-proof."

Rachel blew out the candles and turned on a flashlight. "I have to wait for Daniel," she said, returning to the door. "I promised my brother I wouldn't leave."

She cracked open the door and looked into the front room. She then left the dance studio.

Carlos followed her. He saw the front room was once again free of redbugs. He also saw Helena sprawled across the gym's doorway.

Her eyes were open yet lifeless. Like so many redbug victims, her hands had stiffened into the shapes of claws. Carlos guessed she'd lost her immunity to redbug toxin when she stopped hosting an insect.

Carlos saw his half-eaten tray of ravioli near her body. A few redbugs feasted on the food. Their wings twitched as they fed. Carlos lifted his hose and sprayed the insects.

Rachel stepped over Helena's body and glanced down the dark street. "There will be more swarms," she said. "They often come through town at night, as if they're searching for survivors. Is your team coming for you?"

"I think," Carlos said. His response sounded more like a question.

"You can come with me if you have nowhere to go for the night."

Carlos was grateful for her trust. He asked, "Do you know of a safe shelter around here?"

"My family's house," Rachel said as she picked up Helena's wrists. "That's where I live with my sisters."

Carlos and Rachel carried Helena's body to a small park, where they set the corpse on the bank of a pond. Rachel asked, "I know you didn't know her, but is there anything you'd like to say about her before we leave her? My brother always said it's important to honor the dead."

Carlos shrugged. He wished he could feel more for Helena, but he'd seen enough dead people during his last three tours of duty to become numb to the sight of a corpse. On his first tour, he'd had to help stack bodies that were blocking a hospital corridor. During his second tour, he'd witnessed a pile of burning human remains at a gas station. When he encountered a redbug victim now, he usually found himself thinking, "At least it's not Lucia."

He couldn't remember the last time he'd cried. But according to Vince, the tears came in his sleep.

"I can say something for her," Rachel said. She kneeled by Helena's body and touched the woman's forehead. "May you walk in beauty once you reach the land of the dead."

"I liked that," Carlos said as they lowered Helena into the black water.

Rachel folded her hands over her chest as if she were hugging herself. She watched the partially submerged body. "I think it's a Native American saying. There was this community of women living on a farm outside town. They were into Native American spirituality and healing practices and stuff. They would come into Mirror Lake when people first started dying and the town had to transport bodies to the cemetery. They would say that for the dead people who didn't have family or friends."

Carlos immediately thought of his cousin. "Do you know Lucia Vasquez?" he asked. "I think she might have been part of that community."

"I could have met her," Rachel said. "I visited the community once with my mom. We drove out there so she could try selling some of her hand-knit scarves and sweaters. The women were very kind to us. My mom had a number of buyers."

"Lucia always gravitated toward good people," Carlos said. "She's my cousin." He felt a pang of guilt as he remembered failing to help her up from the floor on the night of the engagement party. He'd been less than a good man that night.

"Can you take me to where those women lived?" he asked. "I need to find her."

"In the morning," Rachel said, starting back toward the street. "I'm afraid my sisters are going to be mad if I stay out all night with a stranger."

Carlos nodded. He wondered how he'd be able to sleep knowing he and Lucia might reunite tomorrow.

Even in the dark, Carlos could see the tarps. The blue material concealed all the three-story house's walls and windows, and portions of it flapped in the nighttime breeze. The only exposed section of the house was the sloping, wood-tiled roof and the chimney protruding from it.

"How do you keep the bugs out of there?" Carlos asked, pointing at the chimney.

"My brother sealed it off," Rachel said. "He said he'd be back long before we need a fire or the fall rains wash the insecticide off the tarps."

"How long has he been gone?"

"Five weeks," she said in a solemn voice.

"And how long does it take to get your sister's camp in Idaho?"

"It's a two-and-a-half-hour drive."

Carlos didn't need to see Rachel's face to recognize her worry or the doubt that her brother would return.

"Your brother could be holed up in a house or a cabin somewhere," he said, "taking care of your sister until the time is right to bring her home."

"That's what I like to think." Rachel walked up a brick path bordered by tall weeds and slid her arm under one of the pieces of tarp.

Carlos heard her knock—three times slowly, then three times quickly.

She motioned for him to join her on the path and asked, "Has your team found many survivors?"

"Eleven," Carlos said, trying to sound enthusiastic about the low number.

Rachel lifted the tarp and led him into a small, pitch-black space outside the front door. Their shoulders touched.

"I hope your cousin survives, too," Rachel said.

Before Carlos could respond, the door cracked open. He could see a glow coming from inside the house.

Something sprayed his suit.

"That's enough, Beth," Rachel soon said.

The door slowly opened further to reveal a pretty teenage girl clutching an insecticide spray can. She wore a white dress that looked too big for her. She had large green eyes and straight red hair that nearly reached her waist. Beyond her was a candlelit living room. Carlos saw the back of a couch, a potted fern that was actually alive, a framed painting of a covered wagon on a golden hill.

Rachel led him by hand inside the house and closed the door behind her. "This is my sister Beth," she told Carlos. "Beth, meet Carlos."

Carlos extended his hand, but the girl didn't receive it. Instead, she turned to Rachel with a sour expression on her face.

"You were supposed to be back an hour ago," she said. "Melanie's been hysterical."

Carlos heard footsteps. He glanced at the staircase near the front door and saw a girl perched on one of the middle stairs. She, too, had lengthy red hair and an ill-fitting white dress, but she looked younger than Beth. Maybe 13 or 14. Her eyes were puffy from crying.

"I thought you'd disappeared like Daniel," Melanie told Rachel.

"You see me now, don't you?" Rachel asked, unzipping the back of her mask. "But I could disappear one day, so it's important for you two to act a little more grown up."

Carlos was stunned when Rachel removed her mask. Thick waves of red hair fell around her gorgeous face. She had large, pouting lips and dimpled cheeks. Her eyes must have been brown, but the candlelight made them look as red as her hair.

Carlos noticed the curves of her breasts and hips beneath the black bodysuit. He guessed she was in her early twenties. He realized he hadn't seen an attractive woman in nearly three weeks.

"Daniel would want us all to be self-reliant," Rachel told her sisters. "Because then he'd be able to trust that we were all right. Don't you think?"

Beth and Melanie offered reluctant nods.

Rachel looked at Beth. "Will you please get Daniel's old bed ready for Carlos?" she asked. "He's going to spend the night tonight."

As Beth climbed the staircase, Melanie watched Rachel expectantly.

Rachel went to the stair where her sister sat and gave her a hug. "Tomorrow's a new day, sweets," she said, and then she sent Melanie upstairs.

She came back down and touched Carlos's shoulder. "You can leave your stuff in the living room."

After setting his extermination hose and backpack next to the couch, Carlos unfastened his helmet and removed his gloves. He was surprised to find he cared about what Rachel thought of his appearance. Once out of the suit, he glanced at his reflection in a mirror on the wall. His black hair had grown out of its buzz cut. The hook-like lines beneath his hazel eyes looked deeper than they ever had before. His cheeks had become flat from his not eating enough on the tour.

He noticed Rachel smiling at him. "Come on," she said. "You look hungry."

She brought him to a candlelit kitchen with a large, square table in its center. She pulled a chair out for him to sit while she lit more candles and removed food items from a cupboard. Carlos eyed the two framed photos propped up on one end of the table. The largest was of a middle-aged blond couple and a little girl standing on the shore of Mirror Lake. The little girl had yellow hair that glowed in the sunlight. The family looked as tranquil as the setting. The adjacent photo was of a red-haired man on a mountainside. He had a slanted grin, and he appeared to be about Rachel's age. Hiking shorts revealed his muscular legs.

"That's everyone who's not here," Rachel said. She set down two bottles of water and their dinner plates, which held assorted nuts, dried fruit, and chunks of chocolate. She sat beside him.

"Sorry I don't have anything hot," she said. "Maybe if we can ever use the chimney again."

Carlos touched her arm. "This is perfect."

Rachel nibbled on a piece of apricot. "Do you have a big family, too?"

"Too much family," Carlos said, looking down at his plate. "I'm not close to them. I've tried to be, but I never quite fit in."

"But you're close to your cousin?"

Carlos recalled Rachel's remarks on the nearby community, and he once again felt relief. Lucia could be just a mile or so away. He wished he could reach her before tomorrow.

"Lucia and I were tight when we were growing up," he said. "I struggled a lot, and she was there for me. I didn't see her as much when we became adults, and then...something came between us. I want us to be close again. Do you mind taking me to the community first thing in the morning?"

"Of course I'll take you," Rachel said, her smiling face glowing in the candlelight.

They ate without speaking for some minutes. Carlos didn't mind the silence. He was comforted by Rachel's presence, and he sensed she was comforted by his.

She eyed the photos on the table. "I know how it is when you really hope to see someone again."

Carlos guessed her hope wasn't laced with the guilt he felt.

"I'll bet you'd like to see your team again, too," Rachel said.

"Not as much as I want to see Lucia."

"Haven't they helped you look for her?"

Carlos shrugged. "Exterminators are supposed to kill bugs. We're not supposed to waste time on anything else. My team leader has made that very clear."

"I like the way you think better," Rachel said. This time she touched his arm. "Besides, the bugs are going to kill us all eventually."

Carlos set down the piece of chocolate he was about to put in his mouth. "I guess all that matters is what we do with the time we have left, then," he said.

Rachel looked deeply into his eyes. "I guess so," she whispered.

Carlos wanted to kiss her even though he barely knew her. He heard someone enter the kitchen. He turned to see Beth standing in the doorway. The teenager folded her arms over her chest.

"His bed's ready now," she told her sister in a flat voice. "I'll take him up to the room."

"Have you eaten enough?" Rachel asked Carlos.

He smiled. "For now. Thank you."

They rose from the table, and Rachel took their plates to the sink. "I'll wake you in the morning and we'll go to the community," she said.

Carlos nodded. "Good night," he said. He began following Beth toward the staircase when he heard Rachel say, "Carlos." He glanced back at her.

She stood at the sink and held up a bottle of water. "Why don't you take one upstairs with you," she said, "in case you get thirsty."

Carlos approached her to receive the bottle. When he neared her, she whispered, "I'm glad you're here."

Carlos smiled. His fingers brushed against hers when he received the water.

Carlos pressed his forehead against the glass of the window. He knew he was in the bedroom Beth had brought him to the night before, yet he could see Lucia and Hector's parents' house directly across the street. There was the porch swing with Aunt Rosita's heart-shaped pillows on it. And the stained-glass basement window a 17-year-old Carlos had forced open the day Lucia taught him how to smoke pot. And the mailbox with the American flag Uncle Lou had painted when the Iran War started.

And there was Azalea's orange VW camper van parked in front of the house. No one sat in the driver's seat.

Carlos watched the house's front door swing open and Lucia stumble across the porch. Her face was pinched with distress. Mascara streaked her cheeks.

Carlos knocked one fist against the glass to gain her attention. "Lucia!" he shouted.

She didn't look up. Once she descended the stairs to the sidewalk, he saw her new expression of rage.

He also saw redbugs dropping out of the sky.

Lucia pulled up her suede fringe jacket over her head to shield herself from the insects.

The clouds poured redbugs, and the insects' gleaming, crimson exoskeletons made a metallic sound as they bounced off the street. They appeared to be lifeless.

Failing to open the passenger's-side door of the van, Lucia stumbled around to the driver's side. She yanked on the handle of the door, but the door wouldn't open for her.

"Lucia!" Carlos called again. His voice was hoarse. "I'm sorry. I know I could have helped you."

Lucia's back was to him as she banged on the driver's-side window. He saw someone rise up behind the steering wheel as if that person had burst through the seat.

It was the dead man Carlos had seen in Azalea's van yesterday.

The burnt-looking corpse in the gray flannel shirt climbed out of the vehicle and slid open the side door for Lucia.

"Don't go!" Carlos screamed. He slammed both fists against the glass, but they made no sound. He only heard the redbugs raining down on the world outside.

After steering Lucia inside the van with one arm, the dead man turned his shrunken head and leered at Carlos from the street.

Despite his sudden fear, Carlos called Lucia's name once more. "I know I should have stopped Hector," he said in a mournful voice.

"Carlos!" The voice was Hector's.

Carlos felt himself weakening. He fell backwards from the window.

"CARLOS!" The voice was Vince's.

Carlos opened his eyes. He was indeed in a bedroom in Rachel's family's house. He lay on a double bed, dressed only in his T-shirt and desert camouflage pants. He saw his uniform and helmet on the rocking chair where he'd placed them the night before. Above the chair was a painting of a Native American woman dipping a bowl in a river.

Carlos glanced at the window he'd peered through in his dream. A blue tarp concealed any view the window would have afforded. Rain pattered the tarp.

"Carlos!" The voice was still Vince's.

Carlos rose from the mattress to try to look outside the window, but he could only see tarp.

The bedroom door opened behind him, and Rachel entered.

She looked as beautiful as she had the night before. She'd tied her red locks on top of her head with a black ribbon. She wore a pale green dress with a belt that accentuated the roundness of her hips. Like Carlos, she was barefoot.

"I think your team is here," she said. Carlos thought he glimpsed disappointment in her eyes.

She led him into the bedroom's closet, which offered a small, circular window that was free of tarp.

Carlos pressed his face against the glass and glanced down at the street in front of the house. He saw his team's Humvee parked in the center of the road. Vince and Noah stood at the start of the path leading to the front door. Both men pointed their extermination hoses at the house. Tyler remained by the Humvee with his arm around his brother. Jared was the one member of the team without uniform or helmet. His skin had changed from a light brown to an ashen color. Bruise-like rings encircled his puffy eyes. His head occasionally lolled as if he were losing consciousness.

Vince pulled from his pocket what must have been his team tracking device. He glanced down at the device and then looked up in Carlos's direction. Carlos figured the only reason Vince had come for him was so the other team members wouldn't report him for abandoning an exterminator.

Carlos stepped back from the window.

"You don't want to see them," Rachel said. She spoke with warmth rather than surprise.

"They're not going to want me to look for my cousin."

"You need to look for her. I've got a truck you can use."

"I don't want to take your guys' vehicle. You may need it."

"We've got a car, too. The truck belongs to the flower shop where I used to work. I drove it home the day the bugs invaded town and I never got a chance to bring it back." Rachel smiled and gave Carlos a reassuring look. "I can distract your team."

Carlos was reluctant about having her cover up his escape. He didn't want Vince disturbing the peace of this household.

"Don't show yourself to them," he said, picking up his socks from his boots. He began to dress. "A tracker chip in my uniform is what led them here. If I leave, they'll leave, too. Is there a way to sneak out of here?"

Rachel nodded. "You can go through the door in the fruit cellar," she said. "The truck is just past the fence in the backyard. You'll drive down the hill until you reach the lake. Then take a right onto Highway 17. Stay on 17 until you see the exit for Sun Rock State Park. That exit will take you to the community. It's called Vision Ranch."

Carlos heard Vince calling for him again as they descended the stairs to the living room. Vince sounded like he was just outside the front door.

Beth and Melanie sat holding each other on the couch. They appeared frightened until they looked at Carlos. Then their eyes flashed resentment.

"Come on," Rachel told Carlos, ignoring her sisters. She hooked her arm around his. She led him through a door and down a dim stairway to the fruit cellar. An electric lantern hung from the ceiling, revealing walls of shelves lined with canned and preserved foods.

"You could live off this for a very long time," Carlos said, wowed by the supplies.

Rachel pressed the truck's key into his hand. "You're going to come back, aren't you?"

Carlos had always known if he found Lucia he would immediately abandon his team and deliver her to a safe place in Seattle. Now he thought if he found her he could come back and talk

Rachel and her sisters into heading west with them. He usually felt disconnected from people he met, but Rachel was different.

"You'll see me again," he said.

She smiled and moved to unlock the back door. She paused and looked at him with eyes that appeared to be tearing.

For the second time, Carlos thought about kissing her. She interrupted this thought by kissing him.

The clouds began to clear as Carlos drove out of town on Highway 17. He was grateful to see the sun illuminate the tan, rolling hills of the high desert. The white boulders and pale green sagebrush distracted him from the occasional crashed or abandoned car he encountered on the way to the Sun Rock State Park exit.

After the truck descended the exit ramp, Carlos spotted a demolished bicycle in the middle of the road. He slowed the truck to see a figure lying near the bicycle. A corpse's blackened arm protruded from the torn sleeve of a Hazard Wrap. Near the figure was a plastic jug that had split open and spilled some congealed yellow substance onto the asphalt.

Carlos pressed his boot on the accelerator pedal and swerved around the dead person. He didn't slow the car until he entered a brown valley containing a farmhouse and a hand-painted roadside sign reading *Vision Ranch.*

Carlos took a left onto the slightly sloping dirt road leading up to the farmhouse. His palms began to sweat inside the gloves of his exterminator suit. He felt light-headed as he imagined the front door of that farmhouse swinging open to reveal Lucia.

On the night of the engagement party, he'd tried to open the front door of his aunt and uncle's house to greet his cousin. But on that occasion Aunt Rosita reached the door first.

And then Hector stomped across the front hallway and grabbed Lucia by the arm. He glared through the doorway toward where Azalea must have been nearing the house.

"Tell her to wait in the car," he told his sister.

"Hector," Lucia said, "She's my-"

"Tell her!"

Carlos was as silent as the rest of the Vasquez clan while Lucia called to her girlfriend and told her to do as Hector asked. Carlos only acted differently from the other Vasquezes when Hector dragged his sister into the guest bedroom. Rather than feign ignorance, Carlos followed the pair into the room.

Inside, Hector was shaking his sister.

"You can be with her behind closed doors," he said, "but not at my engagement party."

"I'm not ashamed." Defiance sharpened Lucia's tone. "I love her."

"Well, I'm ashamed of you," Hector said. "You showing up with her. You dressed like a slut. What's that on your neck?" He moved his hand from her arm to the collar of her suede fringe jacket. He pulled back the collar to reveal a small, purple hickey mark in the shape of a butterfly.

"Hector," Carlos said in a weak voice. "Why don't-"

"I'll bet there are more," Hector said. He yanked open the jacket, and his motion caused Lucia's turquoise dress to tear. A ripped sleeve exposed a bare shoulder.

Lucia's eyes grew wet with tears. She snarled at her brother, "Back the fuck off." She started toward the doorway, shooting Carlos a wounded look. He could see she was disappointed by his failure to defend her.

Hector came behind her and slipped a shiny shoe in front of her so she'd trip. She fell on the hardwood floor with a bang.

Carlos almost reached down to help her stand, but the remembrance of Hector bullying them when they'd been kids paralyzed him. Hector used to drag them down the back stairs of Grandma Milena's house when she was preparing her tortilla soup or talking on the phone.

"Family freaks," Hector would call them.

Hector approached Lucia and placed a foot on her back. "You deserve worse than this," he said.

Carlos remained frozen. He saw that some other family members were peeking inside the door.

Lucia cried out in rage as she lifted herself from beneath her brother's foot. Moving into a standing position, she flashed Carlos a look of loathing. "You've really changed," she hissed.

Before leaving the room, she glared at Hector. "Don't worry," she shouted, "I won't be at anymore family gatherings."

The truck neared the farmhouse. Block-shaped, moss green, and appearing to be decades old, the building was less than hippie-ish. However, after Carlos parked the truck and approached the house, he noticed signs of the community that had lived inside and was hopefully living there still. Little red ribbons fluttered from the lower branches of the poplar trees flanking the two-story structure. A huge dream catcher made of animal hide and black and white feathers dangled from the window ledge directly above the front door. To the right of the house was a collapsed tent constructed out of multi-colored fabrics.

Carlos spotted a Mexican flag in the mix of materials. He recalled how Lucia had worn a tank top bearing that flag to a family barbecue some years ago, and how various relatives had clucked disapproval of the outfit. "She's always trying so hard to be different," Uncle Berto had said with a smirk.

"Lucia!" Carlos called. He was now thrilled to have finally reached his cousin's home. He banged on the door, and, unlike in his dream, the sound of his fist was more than audible. "It's cousin Carlos! I've come for you!"

The door opened to reveal a beautiful, bronze-faced woman with blonde dreadlocks. She wore no protection against redbugs. Her hemp blouse was sleeveless, and her denim shorts only reached the tops of her tanned thighs. On her feet were moccasins.

"Are you one of the naturopaths?" she asked. She stared at Carlos with round eyes that were pale blue and eerily translucent. "We were wondering when you'd return."

"I'm an exterminator," Carlos said, "with Homeland Security. I've come to find my cousin. Her name's Lucia Vasquez."

"Lucia's here," the woman said as if Lucia's presence were obvious. She held out a hand. "I'm Azalea."

Carlos froze—partly because he was stunned he was finally meeting Lucia's significant other, partly because he feared what Lucia might have told her about him. He managed to say, "I'm Carlos," and then he thrust out a gloved hand. He glanced past her, looking for Lucia.

Azalea squeezed his hand weakly. "Welcome to Vision Ranch. Won't you come in?"

"Good idea," Carlos said. "It's not safe out here."

Azalea gave a confused look over his shoulder, as if she were unsure of what he meant. As he entered the front hallway of the house, she said, "We sent Summer and Kuma to town with the salve. They strapped the containers to their bicycles. A couple of the naturopaths were going to test it on themselves. If it worked, they were going to show us how to put it on."

Carlos remembered the words he'd seen on that flyer in Enlightened Choices: *seeking naturopaths to help us find immunity from the bug-*

He considered mentioning the bicycle and body he'd seen on the road, but he was hesitant about delivering what could be crushing news.

"I suppose the world is cured now thanks to that salve," Azalea said. "But I'd still like to see Summer and Kuma come home. Are you one of the naturopaths?"

The repetitive question triggered dread within Carlos. He told himself maybe Azalea was just mentally off from the trauma of the redbug invasion. Maybe she wasn't a nest person. Because if she was a nest person then Lucia could be one, too.

"Lucia's really here?" he asked, peering into Azalea's expressionless eyes.

"I was just going to see her," Azalea said. She closed the front door. "Come with me."

Carlos followed her along a hallway. He wished he could see the back of her neck and ears so he could check for a redbug entry wound, but her dreadlocks concealed her skin.

A sickening syrupy odor filled the house. To the left of Carlos was a staircase bearing dead potted plants and to his right a dim, shuttered room that must have once been a living room. The space now contained a circle of folding chairs and meditation cushions. In its center was a shadowy table resembling an altar. Carlos saw framed photographs and a small marble statue of a woman on the altar.

"Wait," Azalea said. She reeled around to face Carlos. "I think I hear her in the driveway. She borrowed my van to do some errands. She must be back."

Carlos didn't hear anything. He pictured Azalea's VW camper van in the desert, where his team had left it. All the van's tires had been flat. He watched Azalea return to the front door and open it. She peered out at the quiet morning and called, "Lucia?"

Then she stepped outside and shut the door behind her.

Carlos hurried into the living room to open shutters and look out at his cousin. As he neared the altar, he saw the marble figure was a bare-chested woman wielding a bow and arrow. The picture frames held images of what looked like female deities. One was a Buddha-like woman sitting cross-legged on a circular cluster of flowers. The other was an angry-faced, dark blue-skinned woman with four arms. In one of her hands was a sword. In another, a man's decapitated head.

Carlos shivered. He saw a streak of orange, glistening egg sacs across the yellow silk cloth of the altar. A redbug emerged from behind the frame that displayed the rage-filled deity and flew upwards to the ceiling.

Carlos scowled.

Covering the entire ceiling was a network of redbug nests. Carlos saw insects clinging to various egg sacs. The redbugs could have been young insects or females preparing to lay more eggs. Carlos regretted leaving his extermination hose in the truck. He was only going to bring it into the house if no one was home and he had to break inside.

A knock sounded at the front door.

"Can someone let us in?" Azalea called.

Carlos raised his eyebrows when he heard the "us." "Us" as in Azalea and Lucia. Lucia as in his living and breathing cousin.

The knock sounded on the farmhouse's front door again.

Carlos's hand trembled as he turned the doorknob. "Lucia?" he asked.

Azalea stood outside. She was alone.

"Where's Lucia?" Carlos asked. "You said 'us.'"

"I was just going to see her," Azalea said, stepping through the front door. She gazed blankly ahead of her and moved through the hallway once again. "Come with me."

Carlos tried not to be annoyed by her crazy behavior.

Just after they passed the living room, Azalea paused. She turned back toward Carlos. "Wait," she said, "I think I hear her."

"No," Carlos said in a firm voice. He reached for her shoulders to steer her toward her original destination. "Not again." As soon as he touched her he spotted the reddish swelling on the left side of her neck.

The sign of the insect inside her.

"You were going to see Lucia," Carlos said as if he were a therapist and Azalea his patient. He motioned toward the end of the hallway. "She must be back there somewhere."

"Yes," Azalea said as if she were remembering.

They entered a cavernous, sunlit kitchen. On one counter was a row of plastic jugs similar to the one Carlos had seen on the road. All the jugs were uncapped, and they had the same yellow, viscous contents. Carlos stepped closer to the containers and noticed the syrupy odor intensified to an almost unbearable level. He thought the yellow substance looked familiar, and then he remembered what redbug guts looked like.

"The salve comes from the insects?" he asked Azalea.

She didn't respond. She moved to the other side of the kitchen, next to a table holding a pile of dried white roses. She was assembling a bouquet from the flowers.

"Azalea," Carlos said. "Where is Lucia?"

Azalea looked in his direction and smiled dreamily. She appeared to be in a trance. She tied a red ribbon around the roses and asked, "Do you hear her, too?"

Holding the bunch of flowers, she opened the kitchen door and descended wooden steps to the backyard.

Carlos shadowed her. Weeds and wildflowers choked the yard, which stretched until the bottom of a brown hill. As Azalea entered the tangled growth, Carlos noticed large sticks protruding from various parts of the yard. Someone had attached feathers and beads and even crystals to those sticks.

Azalea approached one stick that had bright blue feathers on its shaft.

Carlos recalled the blue feathers that had been in Lucia's hair on the night of the engagement party.

"No," he whispered. A burning grief filled the pit of his stomach as he read the letters carved down the length of a grave marker.

L

U

C

I

A

Carlos couldn't breathe. He watched Azalea kneel and prop the roses against the base of the stick.

She looked up at him and offered another smile. "Lucia's everywhere," she said in a simultaneously comforting and vacant voice.

Carlos turned away from her. Stinging tears ran down his cheeks. There was no way to dry his eyes without removing his helmet. He ran around the side of the house toward the truck, his sobs ripping through the silence of the ranch.

Once again on the freeway, Carlos wiped the tears from his eyes. He had the idea he could let go of the steering wheel and slam his boot against the accelerator pedal. The truck would veer to the side of Highway 17, break through the rickety-looking railing, and shoot off a cliff overlooking a stretch of the Columbia River.

But then he thought of Rachel. Though the discovery of Lucia's death had dissolved his sense of purpose, he still desired to see that woman who'd kissed him this morning.

The woman who was waiting for him to return to Mirror Lake.

As Carlos drove up the hill leading to Rachel's house, he wondered how he could have missed seeing his team's Humvee on the drive back into town. He'd been sure the team would come after him—unless Vince had decided not to pursue him so far outside Mirror Lake. Carlos figured the team had probably returned to one of the lakeside houses the twins had debugged yesterday.

He parked the truck on the same weedy stretch of street where he'd found it. After leaving the vehicle with his extermination hose, he climbed over the peeling white fence bordering Rachel's backyard. He felt somewhat calm once again as he waded through the tall, sunlit grass and dandelions of the yard. He glanced up at the tarp-covered house and imagined Rachel and her sisters sharing a peaceful lunch inside.

Then he heard a girl screaming.

Carlos saw the back door through which he'd exited in the morning no longer had a tarp covering it. The blue material lay on the brick walkway and revealed dirty boot prints. Someone had smashed the door's window.

Nervous, he turned the door's handle and entered the fruit cellar. The cans and jars lining the shelves all seemed intact. But then he spotted the few redbugs clinging to the electric lantern in the center of the ceiling.

The screaming started again.

Carlos bounded up the stairs until he reached a locked door. He pounded on it and hollered, "Rachel!"

Someone unlocked the door and pulled it open. Wearing helmet and suit, Noah stared back at Carlos. "There you are," Noah said with a look of relief. "I was worried the bugs got you."

A whimpering sound came from the living room. Carlos pushed past Noah to locate the source of the noise, and then he froze.

Beth lay on the couch. Her long locks of red hair were spilled across a cushion, and her skin was a sickly white. Tyler sat near her bare feet. Like Noah, he wore his full exterminator uniform. Beth squinted her eyes as Tyler inserted a C-99 syringe into her neck.

"We didn't know who was in the house," Noah said, sounding regretful. "Vince thought you were in here, but then your signal faded. Vince was suspicious of all the tarps. He said someone must be trying to keep people out. He wanted to know why."

Beth whimpered again and moved her head from side to side. Carlos saw the wet, red mark beneath her chin.

A redbug entry wound.

"You let the insects inside," Carlos said, his anger apparent. He glanced around the living room and saw blue clumps of insecticide foam on one wall. The foam concealed the painting of the covered wagon. It stuck to the potted fern, which had tipped over and spilled soil onto a rug.

"Where's Rachel?" Carlos said, glancing back at Noah.

Noah pointed upwards. "In one of the bedrooms. She had a bad reaction to the C-99."

Carlos rushed up the staircase to the second floor. He spotted Vince at the end of the hallway, pacing back and forth in what appeared to be a master bedroom. Vince didn't look at Carlos. He was staring at the floor.

Carlos headed toward his team leader until he noticed the figures in a bedroom to his right.

The room must have been Beth and Melanie's. The walls were covered in floral wallpaper, posters of pop bands, and a large watercolor painting of a red-haired man resembling the girls' brother, Daniel.

Melanie stood between the beds, wearing a Hazard Wrap that was too big for her. She stared down at Rachel, who lay on one of the beds with her eyes closed and swollen. Beads of sweat speckled her forehead. She still wore the green dress she'd had on this morning. Jared lay on the other bed. Skin necrosis had set in, turning much of his flesh a purplish gray. His gaunt cheeks and bulging, desperate eyes made him look ghoulish.

"Hey, buddy," Jared spoke in a raspy voice. "I'll bet we're a sight."

Carlos tried to summon a smile for his team member. He propped his extermination hose against the wall and approached Melanie. He squeezed her shoulder. "Beth could use your company downstairs. I'll stay with Rachel and make sure she's okay."

Melanie hesitated and then, with a sigh, she left the room. Carlos sat on the mattress. He touched one of Rachel's bare legs. She looked as if she were attempting to open her eyes.

"We broke in through the back door," Jared said. "She came down the basement stairs and told us to get out of her house. She and Vince argued, and that was when the bugs flew in through the broken window. One of them went right into her neck."

Carlos reached for Rachel's chin and gently turned her head. He saw the already-scabbing entry wound on the left side of her neck, just below her earlobe. He felt like he wouldn't be able to handle finding and feeling the insect beneath her skin.

"Some other bugs landed on her," Jared said, "so Vince decided to give her C-99 to be safe. The middle sister was in the same situation. Only the youngest avoided the bugs."

Carlos used a bed sheet to dab Rachel's sweaty forehead.

"You do know her, don't you?" Jared asked. "She denied it, but the middle sister made a comment about how they didn't want 'more exterminators' in their house."

Carlos nodded. "She watched out for me."

"You need to be careful of Vince," Jared said. "He's kind of-"

"Kind of what?" The voice was Vince's.

Carlos turned around to see his team leader looming in the doorway.

"You've decided to rejoin the flock," Vince said, a sneer visible behind the faceplate of his helmet. "Where'd you go?"

"Why'd you bring the team in here?" Carlos asked, feeling that familiar loathing for Vince. "Rachel told you to leave the house."

"We had to find a certain missing member who's been ever so valuable to us. His name's Carlos Vasquez. He led us here."

Carlos went quiet. He recognized it was ultimately his fault the team was in this house and a redbug was in Rachel. He once again watched her unconscious figure.

"I'm afraid we're all in this shit storm together," Vince said.

Carlos looked up and saw Vince staring bleakly at the tarp covering the bedroom window.

"I heard from the Director of Teams again," Vince continued. "He said the team is no longer. Disbanded. 'Don't call us, we'll call you.' Apparently, things in Seattle are so bad the higher-up's have no time to manage us. Or provide us with gasoline. The Director said we need to find our own way back to the city."

Carlos imagined the current state of chaos in western Washington. He thought of his family again, and what they must be suffering. But the death of Lucia prevented him from feeling anything too acutely. And he was more concerned about Rachel.

"Don't worry, though," Vince said. "I've got a plan for us all. I'm going to tell it to everyone over lunch." He went to help Jared sit up in bed.

Carlos tried squeezing Rachel's fingers, but she failed to respond. He knew she wasn't strong enough to go downstairs and eat.

As Vince led a limping Jared out of the room, he told Carlos, "You've never been hard enough for this job. I've always known that."

Carlos didn't want to give Vince his attention. Rather than look at his team leader, he kept his eyes on Rachel.

"But I guess that doesn't matter anymore," Vince said, "because our only job now is survival."

Carlos watched Noah finish nailing the pieces of broken chair over the back door's shattered window. He and Noah had come down to the fruit cellar to fully secure the house before lunch.

Noah struck the final nail with the hammer a few times, and Carlos pictured Lucia's grave marker in the dirt behind the farmhouse. He thought of Rachel upstairs, feverish and probably just a couple days away from entering the ground herself.

"You kill them all?" Noah asked.

Carlos gave him a startled look.

"The bugs," Noah said, pointing at the insecticide foam dripping from the ceiling. "You sprayed them, right?"

"Yes. The house should be clear except-"

Again, he thought of Rachel and the bug nestled under some part of her skin.

"The nest people," Noah said in a solemn voice.

"Rachel and Beth," Carlos said as a correction.

Noah offered an apologetic look. "You really connected with her—with Rachel," he said.

Carlos didn't respond. He said, "We should head upstairs."

"You know," Noah said, "Tyler told me there have been cases of nest people who didn't lose their...faculties. They seem normal. They just have bugs living under their skin."

Carlos felt hope rising within him. He waited for Noah to say more.

"But what do we really know?" Noah added. "Vince says nest people are no longer human. He calls them 'bug bombs.' He said Helena was a bug bomb."

"They're human," Carlos said. He noticed Noah's cross had disappeared from his suit. "You shouldn't always listen to Vince."

Noah barely nodded. He started up the stairs. "I used to be so sure we'd win this war against the bugs and I'd come home to my wife," he said. "Now I don't even know where she is."

"Welcome to the last supper, my boys," Vince said.

Carlos watched him enter the kitchen carrying a six-pack of bottled beer. He set the containers on the table and grinned down at the platter of peanuts, dried strawberries, beef jerky, and chocolate squares Noah had assembled.

"I don't know if I'd call this a lunch," he said, "but it's a start."

Carlos frowned as Vince lifted his faceplate and popped one of the chocolate squares into his mouth. Carlos resented his team leader for depleting the girls' food supply.

"I guess I should be more aware of my surroundings," Vince said, pulling down his faceplate. He went to the kitchen doorway and glanced in the direction of where Melanie tended to Beth on the couch. He shut the door. "After all, there are still bugs in the house."

He returned to the table and lowered himself into the chair across from Carlos. Noah sat on another side of the table, and the twins were across from him. Tyler kept his arm around Jared, who was trembling because he had the chills.

Jared reached for some strawberries with a shaky hand. Tyler had to place the fruit between his brother's lips.

"Jared and I are heading back to Seattle after this," Tyler announced to the group. "I'm going to check him into Harborview Medical Center. I heard they've been doing research on bug toxin there. They might have some better treatment options by now."

Carlos glanced at Vince and saw he was nodding.

"I thought you said the Humvee didn't have enough gas to get back to Seattle," Carlos said.

"It doesn't," Vince said, not looking him in the eyes. "But the truck you drove today does. Isn't that right, Noah?"

Noah gave Carlos a guilty look, and then he stared down at the peanuts in the palm of his hand. "It has enough gas," he said. "I checked like you asked me to."

"You can't just take the girls' truck," Carlos said. He didn't mention they also had a car.

Vince finally met Carlos's gaze with a stone-cold stare. "Let's be realistic," he said. "Those girls aren't going anywhere."

"They could recover," Carlos said. "Like Jared." He regretted his statement when he saw the doomed look on Jared's wasting face.

"The youngest will be fine," Vince said. "Melanie's her name? She'll sit between Tyler and Jared when they go back to Seattle."

"You can't separate the sisters," Carlos said.

"I can do whatever the hell I want," Vince shouted. He slammed a fist on the table, causing some of the food to fall off the platter. "My team may be disbanded, but I'm still the goddamn leader here. I should never have let you compromise my position."

The rest of the team was silent as Vince opened a bottle of beer and guzzled the alcohol. He set the half-empty container on the table and looked at Carlos again. "Besides," he said. "You don't have to worry about Melanie. You'll be going with her—but in the back of the truck."

"Oh, yeah?" Carlos asked, defiance in his voice. "And what about you?"

"I'm going to stay in this house with Noah. There's plenty of food and supplies for us here. And then Tyler's going to come back in the next few days with enough gas for the Humvee."

"This is Rachel and her sisters' house," Carlos said.

"Not anymore it ain't. Listen, Carlos, I've made these decisions for everyone's good."

Carlos glanced at Noah and the twins to see if any of them sided with him. They all stared dumbly at the platter.

"I'm not leaving Rachel," he said.

Vince shook his head and offered Carlos a crooked grin. He said, "And what if I told you Rachel asked that you go?"

"You've got everything?" Carlos asked when Melanie appeared at the top of the staircase. She descended the stairs in a Hazard Wrap and set her small suitcase by the front door. She shot him a spiteful look and went to Beth again.

Carlos wondered if Melanie would put on another show of resistance. The last one ended with Vince picking up the shrieking and weeping teenager and carrying her upstairs to pack her clothes.

"We're going to take you to a safer place," Carlos said. He tried to sound earnest when he added, "We'll make sure you see your sisters again," but his words sounded hollow.

Melanie hugged Beth, whose sweating body was propped up against a pile of pillows on the couch. Beth's face was swollen and red, and she was barely able to wrap an arm around her sister. Pained by the sight, Carlos went outside the front door to watch the rest of his team loading the truck with supplies from the Humvee.

Jared sat in the passenger's seat of the truck. Vince and Tyler carried a canister of insecticide to the truck bed. Noah walked toward Carlos. The oncoming evening caused the sky to turn a reddish pink. Carlos thought he saw a flock of birds rising then swooping over the horizon.

Or perhaps it was a swarm of redbugs.

"I would go in your place if I could," Noah told him in a quiet voice. "But Vince wants me to be here with him. I don't think he's ready for Seattle yet. He's nursing his ego after the higher-up's cut him off from extermination service."

"So you'll stay in this house and nurse Vince's ego while those girls die."

"You don't know that they're going to die," Noah said.

"I won't know anything about them if I'm going to Seattle."

Noah touched his arm. "This is for the best, Carlos. You and Vince need to be miles apart. You can't be around each other without clashing."

"And you just lie right down for him," Carlos seethed. He remembered Lucia on the bedroom floor, and how he'd refrained from reaching out to her. He wondered if she would have still ended up in eastern Washington if he'd lifted her from the floor. Sensing the approach of another wave of sorrow, he started back to the house.

He paused to ask Noah, "What did you do with your cross?"

Noah hesitated before answering, "I don't know what I believe in anymore."

"Neither do I," Carlos said.

Carlos cracked open the door to see Rachel's prone figure in the dim bedroom. He lit the candle on the table by her bed and sat on the mattress. He removed one glove to touch her damp forehead.

He was relieved to see her open her eyes slightly.

"Melanie told me you're going with her," she said in a whisper. "That's what I wanted."

"I want to be here with you," he said. "Melanie could stay-"

"She needs to go. Beth and I can't take care of her any longer." Rachel struggled to swallow, and then she said, "It's even more dangerous for her to be here now. Will you please watch out for her?"

"Yes," Carlos said, his voice betraying his reluctance. He hated leaving Rachel with Vince.

Rachel looked toward one of the room's dark walls. "Daniel's not coming back."

"You don't know that," Carlos said.

Rachel nodded. "I do know. It's okay."

"My cousin Lucia," Carlos said, his voice cracking, "she's dead."

Rachel peered into his eyes sympathetically. "The bugs can't bother them anymore," she said. "Daniel and Lucia. And the bugs won't be able to bother me."

Carlos squeezed her hand. He almost let it go when he felt it was in the shape of a claw. "I'm coming back for you," he said. "I'll make sure Melanie's in a place where people will take care of her, and then I'll come back."

"Don't," Rachel said. "You don't need to see me after I'm gone."

"You don't know what's going to happen," Carlos said.

"We both know how this will end. Death is the way of the world now."

"Haven't you left yet?"

Carlos heard the question when he reached the bottom of the staircase. He turned around to see Vince standing by the door leading to the fruit cellar. Vince had both hands behind his back.

"I'm going now," Carlos said. He fetched his extermination hose from the rear of the couch where Beth slept. Surprisingly, her face had become more pink than red. Carlos wondered if the C-99 had helped her symptoms, or if it was something else. He thought he saw a bulge in the side of her neck. Knowing there was nothing he could do about the insect within that bulge, he started toward the front door.

"Good luck," Vince said. He now leaned against the railing of the staircase. "Everyone's going to need it."

Carlos nodded. He headed toward the front door again when he felt that searing hatred inside him. He opened the door and, despite evening's dimness, he saw that Jared, Melanie, and Tyler were all in the truck. Noah stood by the idling vehicle, watching something in the distance.

Carlos looked in the same direction and realized that the distant flock of birds he'd seen earlier really was a swarm of redbugs.

The insects were getting closer.

He was about to walk through the doorway when he glanced back into the house and saw Vince mounting the stairs with a roll of duct tape in one hand.

"Hey," Noah called to Carlos from outside. "You guys should get going. Bugs are coming."

Carlos held up a hand, signaling for his team to wait. Noah started yelling for him to get into the truck.

Carlos silently closed the door and climbed the stairs. He still carried his extermination hose.

He pushed open the door to the candlelit bedroom and saw Rachel now lay on her stomach. The sheet that had covered her was pulled back to the tops of her thighs. Her hair was positioned to the right of her head so her neck was exposed.

Vince sat on the bed and brought a strip of duct tape toward the exposed skin.

"What are you doing?" Carlos asked, moving toward the mattress.

"Making sure the bug stays inside her," Vince said. "Now get the hell out of here like you were supposed to."

Carlos pictured Hector yanking open Lucia's jacket. He heard the tearing of her dress.

His face went hot inside his helmet. "Don't touch her," he told Vince.

Vince made a motion to shoo Carlos away. He brought the duct tape closer to Rachel's skin.

"Stop!" Carlos shouted. He dropped his extermination hose and lunged at Vince, shoving him face forward toward the wall. Vince's helmet smashed against the wall and made a cracking sound.

He turned toward Carlos with a broken faceplate and a look of rage. A shard of the faceplate had cut one of his cheeks. "I should have left you to die in the desert!" he hollered, and then he lifted himself from the mattress to charge at Carlos.

Carlos avoided Vince's rushing form, and his team leader fell onto the empty bed. Carlos's anger and adrenaline sent a single thought coursing through his head: *Get Vince out of the house.*

He picked up his extermination hose and began spraying. The foam entered Vince's helmet, and he started howling.

Carlos hooked his arm around Vince's and forced him out of the bedroom and down the staircase. As they went, Vince scooped the toxic foam off his face.

Carlos saw Beth sitting up on the couch with a look of curiosity in her puffy eyes.

"I'm going to get cancer because of you," Vince said in a crazed voice.

Carlos shook his head. "None of us is going to live long enough to get cancer." He steered Vince toward the front door. "You're leaving now. This house belongs to Rachel and her sisters."

Vince wiped more of the insecticide's blue moisture from his eyes. He blinked repeatedly and glanced around him. Carlos guessed the insecticide had temporarily blinded him.

"Don't you understand?" Vince asked, glaring at a wall instead of Carlos. "Those girls are fucking insects."

"I know who the insect is," Carlos said, and then he pulled open the front door.

At first, he thought Noah was pushing on the door to get inside. But then he saw the red glimmer of the exoskeletons that poured inside the house.

A swarm filled the entire living room. The redbugs caused the electric lanterns hanging from the ceiling to sway violently, and soon they began to fall.

Carlos saw Beth press her hands against the side of her head. She screamed.

"Curl up into a ball and cover your face!" he called to her.

He turned to Vince. A layer of writhing bugs was where his faceplate had been.

The last of the lanterns dropped, and Carlos was in blackness with the eerie hum of the insects, Beth's whimpering, and Vince's groaning.

Carlos went down onto his hands and knees. He kept his faceplate close to the floor for protection from the swarm. He crawled in the direction of where he thought the staircase was, and soon he was climbing the stairs.

An incessant hum from above indicated that the insects had invaded the second floor as well.

Carlos moved as quickly as possible along the hallway, and then he felt the break in the wall that marked the doorway to the bedroom where Rachel had been. He rose to his knees after entering the room and slammed the door shut. The candles had gone out, leaving the room in darkness. Carlos no longer heard the insects' hum, but he sensed there were redbugs in here.

He heard their legs tapping against the windowpane.

He climbed onto the bed and felt Rachel's still figure next to him. *Please don't let her be dead,* he repeated in his head.

One of Rachel's legs shifted.

"It's me," Carlos whispered. "Carlos."

"You came back already," Rachel said in a soft voice.

"For good," Carlos said. He slipped his hand under the sheet and traced the length of her bare arm until he reached her hand.

It was no longer in the shape of a claw.

BOOK 2
NIGHT NURSE

LATE SUMMER

Tess sat up on the couch when she heard the electronic trumpeting signaling she had a text message. She quickly shut her Biology 200 textbook and retrieved her cell phone from the coffee table. She hoped she was finally receiving a reply to the message she'd sent her mother this afternoon:

> *I haven't heard from you in days. The news*
> *said the bugs are getting closer to the mountains.*
> *Please tell me you're safe.*

She frowned when she saw the new message was from her friend James. The text read:

> *im in yr apt building*

A banging sounded at the front door of the three-bedroom apartment Tess shared with her mother.

Tess peered through the peephole and saw James standing in the hallway. She was surprised to see him wearing a surgical mask and blue scrubs. He'd flattened and parted his usually spiky black hair. He brought his face closer to the door until one of his green eyes was on the other side of the peephole. "Evening, Nurse Fenston," he said. "I know you're in there."

Tess opened the door and asked, "What the hell have you got on?"

James gently pushed his way into the apartment with a black leather doctor's bag. He pulled down the surgical mask. "I'd like to ask you that question."

Tess folded her arms over her chest, suddenly self-conscious of the plaid pajamas she'd worn since this morning. She'd been studying for her upcoming biology exam all day. Her dark brown hair was still tied on top of her head in a messy bun.

"It's after 9," she said. "What am I supposed to be wearing?"

"It's a Saturday night in Seattle," James said, setting the doctor's bag on the coffee table. He unzipped the bag and removed a white nurse uniform and cap. "You should be dressed for dancing at Nightweb."

Tess gave a sarcastic laugh. "Right," she said. "Like I'm going clubbing tonight."

She shook her head and grinned as she watched James lift two energy drinks and a bottle of vodka from his bag. She remembered how they'd gone on a few dates after meeting in a psychology class at Seattle Central Community College last winter. They were both 20 at the time and interested in eventually entering the medical field—he as a pharmacist, she as a nurse. But by the third date, they realized they weren't romantically compatible. He wanted to dance to techno, she wanted to see life-affirming films. He revealed he was into girls who gave him "a few good slaps" in bed, she admitted she'd only slept with one guy—her high school boyfriend.

They did have the chemistry for a friendship, however. Tess wasn't sure exactly why, but James explained it as they shared a Vietnamese sandwich near campus one day. "We're both neurotic as hell," he'd said.

"Am I really such a head case?" Tess asked, blushing. She remembered how she'd had to drop out of Washington State University because of her concentration problems and those incessant panic attacks.

James patted her shoulder. "You've got your death-of-a-parent issues and I've got my addiction issues."

Tess now reluctantly fetched two glasses from one of the kitchen cabinets. She opened the freezer and grabbed a handful of ice cubes. "I can't go out with you tonight," she said, depositing the ice in the glasses. She brought the glasses to James. "I'm still waiting to hear from my mom. And I've got to study."

"I'm worried about you," James said as he mixed the drinks. "Ever since your mom left for eastern Washington you spend nearly all your time at home. You're 21, not 61." He handed Tess her glass.

She stared into the fluorescent pink liquid and thought of her mother saying, "You're my daughter, Tess, not my mother. You don't have to worry about me. The government sends hundreds of exterminators into the quarantine zone each week, and nearly all of them return perfectly healthy. And I won't be chasing bugs. I'll just be testing soil. I'll come home soon enough so you can keep an eye on me again."

Tess sipped the liquid and felt it burn her throat. A warm feeling expanded from her gut and seeped into her limbs. Alcohol had never caused such a reaction in her. She looked at James and asked, "How can I relax when people are dying from bugs landing on their skin? The world seems to be falling apart."

James finished his drink and refilled the glass with a little bit of energy drink and a lot of vodka. He shrugged. "Everyone thinks the world is going to end about every 10 years. Remember 2012? Or when the robins went extinct? Or the Christmas Bomb threats? Besides, the redbugs are east of the Cascades and we're west, where it's too damp and cold for their liking."

"My mom's east of the Cascades," Tess said. She took a second, larger sip of her drink. She noticed James had gone quiet.

"Sorry," he finally said, giving her a guilty look. He topped off her glass with vodka. "You said she's doing testing around those

Homeland Security walls? I'm sure the government will protect her."

Tess nodded before drinking more. Her mother was testing how the insecticide-spraying walls affect the environment. She recalled her mother criticizing the construction of the barriers.

"Redbugs are a sign it's time for us to have a better understanding of other species," her mother had said. "We shouldn't be raising toxic walls that will harm all kinds of species—including our own."

The drink was making Tess feel as if her entire body had developed a layer of fuzz. She set her glass on the table and touched one of her cheeks. "It's like the skin of a tennis ball," she told James with a chuckle.

"Just think how good that nurse uniform is going to feel," he said. He handed her the outfit, and as she fingered the soft cotton her previous resistance seemed silly. She went into the kitchen to change. She untied her hair and allowed its wavy strands to drop to her shoulders.

"I feel like my brain is wrapped in bubble gum," she said when she returned to the living room in the nurse's uniform. "Is something wrong with me, doctor?" she asked with a laugh.

"Maybe," James said. He stood staring at the series of framed photographs on one wall. The photographs featured women in black burkas. All the subjects were in front of decimated buildings in Tehran. Tess's mother had taken the pictures when the University of Washington sent her to test how much the chemical soldiers' attacks had increased toxicity levels in Iran.

"Cool art," James said.

"I think they're bizarre," Tess said, laughing again. "My mom took them right after the Iran War ended."

"What's their meaning?"

"You should ask my mom," Tess said, glancing around for her cell phone. She vaguely remembered she was waiting to hear from her mother. "Something about how we fool ourselves with our attempts at self-protection?"

She looked at herself in a mirror to adjust the nurse's cap on her head. She admired the cap's little red cross, which had begun to glow. Her blue irises seemed to be growing, making her eyes appear cartoonish. She saw that the nurse's skirt barely covered her thighs. She touched the bony knob of one knee and felt it tingle.

"You look hot," James said.

Tess turned to him. "I feel like I'm on fire," she said, "and I don't mind the flames." She gave a hysterical laugh, and James did the same.

Tess embraced him. "What's wrong with me, doctor?" she whispered.

"I sprinkled some EZ in our drinks."

"You drugged me?" Tess had an idea she should be angry, but she forgot how to summon that emotion. Part of her was grateful someone had taken her out of her usual state of worry.

"You needed the medicine," James said, separating from her and fetching her cell phone and purse.

Tess smiled as she received her belongings and dropped the phone inside the purse. She didn't check the phone for a new text message. She led James toward the door and announced, "It's Webnight!"

Tess was sitting next to James on the light rail train when she began feeling dizzy. The train had just left First Hill, where Tess and her mother lived, and was entering downtown Seattle. Tess noticed the streetlamps and building lights all had pulsating halos around them. She blinked her eyes with the hope she would once again have clear vision, but the rapid movement of her eyelids only made her dizzier—and nauseous.

"I want to get off," she told James. "I think I'm going to be sick."

He gave her a concerned look. "There's a stop coming up. You'll feel better if you get some fresh air. We can walk the rest of the way to the club."

Tess soon dashed from the train to the side of a building with a billboard warning:

You're always prepared for rain, Seattle.
Be prepared for worse.

HAZARD WRAPS – available in all sizes

Tess vomited on a strip of weeds while James held her nurse's cap for her.

"EZ isn't the perfect drug," he said. "It doesn't last that long, and sometimes your first dose can make you puke. But it gets better with the second try. I'm hoping to score more in the club." He removed the bottle of vodka from his doctor's bag and held it out to her. "There's a little left. Finish it off. It'll revive the good effects."

Tess reluctantly took the bottle and drank some of the alcohol. She was grateful they were on a quiet block with no one around. But as she took another swig, she noticed a man standing directly across the street from them, just outside the empty, brightly lit lobby of a corporate office tower. He had long, matted gray hair and a soiled face. He was wrapped in a tattered quilt, and he held a cardboard sign in front of him. Tess was unable to read the handwriting on the sign.

"Maybe we should just go back to my house," she told James in a nervous voice. "I might get sick again."

"You'll be fine," James said, guiding the bottle toward her lips. "You just need one more tablet of EZ and you'll be set for the night. Then you'll eat a candy bar before bed and you'll wake up feeling like you spent the night dutifully studying at home."

Tess felt that magical warmth returning to her body. Her dizziness and nausea had faded. She decided not to chastise James for spiking her drink. She finished off the vodka and shrugged her shoulders. "You're the doctor, right?" she asked.

"And you're my nurse." James took the empty bottle and tossed it under the billboard. The glass shattered, and the many shards seemed to twinkle on the concrete. "Whoops," he said with a laugh.

Tess laughed, too, even though she'd never found littering amusing. She became quiet when she noticed the man with the cardboard sign now stood on the curb behind James. The man silently stared at them with a wide-eyed look of insanity.

Tess read the words on the sign:

INSECTS SHALL INHERIT THE EARTH
WE'VE JUST GOT OUR SOULS

James turned around to see what had snagged Tess's attention. "Lighten up, mister," he snapped. He grabbed Tess's hand and pulled her downhill in the direction of the club.

Tess turned back toward the man while she was setting the nurse's cap on her head. Her eyes met his crazy gaze, and she felt a pang of fear despite the artificial reassurance the drug sent through her veins.

"Yeah, lighten up," she tried to shout, but her voice came out a whisper.

"Listen to the boom," Tess said in awe. She placed her hand on the building's cement wall and felt the vibration of the electronic music. Tess thought if she didn't hear the beat of the music she'd never guess there was a club inside this drab, utilitarian structure that was located beneath a freeway ramp dividing the Pioneer Square and SoDo neighborhoods.

James pressed his back against the vibrating wall and inhaled slowly and sensuously. "Feels like sex," he said with a smile.

If she'd been sober, Tess would have glanced away from him with flushed cheeks. But tonight she stared back at him with a feeling of intrigue. She wondered what would happen if she asked him to spend the night with her.

A trio of men in robot costumes passed by and pulled open the club's nondescript door.

James motioned for Tess to follow the robots. "You're going to be a whole new woman after this," he told her.

"I already feel like one," she said, pinching her numb chin to make sure ordinary reality wasn't returning too soon.

Tess sensed she was floating as she climbed the dark staircase leading to the club. She paused halfway up to stare at her shadowy face in a scratched mirror panel. "That's not me," she spoke aloud to herself. She began laughing again. Her body felt like a sack of jelly.

James squeezed her arm. "We're almost in the operating room, Nurse Fenston."

The space that housed Nightweb was like some enchanted cave Tess had read about in her Greek & Roman Literature class. Dark bodies writhed in a mass on the dance floor while spirit-like lights blinked turquoise, violet, fuchsia, and red above their heads. The music continued its penetrating booming, and lyrics occasionally filled the room:

I'm electric 'lectric human
I'm electric 'lectric ghost

Tess noticed a few platforms that rose above the dancers. Three women in costumes strutted on the platform that was closest to her. One woman was dressed as a ladybug, another a butterfly, the third a bee.

"Almost everyone here is wearing a costume," Tess shouted over the music at James, who was paying their entry fees to a man sitting at a folding table. The man's face was covered in tattoos.

"Nightweb's a place for people to get freaky," James shouted back at her. "Now I'm going to find some EZ so we don't become dull."

They pushed through the jerking and swaying bodies, and Tess danced as they traversed the floor. Occasionally, people pressed against her, making it difficult to move or breathe. But James managed to lead her all the way across the space to a windowed back wall.

"I'm heading out there," James said, pointing out one window at a large, crowded deck that was connected to the club. Beyond the deck were the silhouettes of more industrial buildings and, above those, the glow of the I-5 freeway. A reddish-orange harvest moon loomed in the sky.

"Be back soon," James told Tess. "Stay by this window, okay?"

Tess nodded. She watched him force his way through a wall of sweaty torsos, and soon she saw him reappear on the outdoor staircase leading to the deck.

Tess looked back at the dance floor and found herself moving to the music once again. *You see?* she told herself. *You don't always have to be such a worrywart. You can let go like other people do.*

As she watched her fellow dancers, the blinking lights began to form halos around them. Tess's dizziness returned. She turned toward the window to locate James, but a man blocked her view.

"What a night," he shouted at her.

Tess lost her drug-induced calm when she saw the bandages covering the man's body. She remembered her teary-eyed mother telling her when she was 17, "I don't think you should come to the hospital to see your father. The bike accident made him unrecognizable. He's all wrapped up in gauze."

"But what if I don't go and…something else happens to him?" Tess had asked.

"What a night!" the man repeated in an even louder voice.

Tess recognized he was dressed as a mummy. She shook off the thoughts of her father's passing. "Yes," she hollered. "It's a real spectacle."

She felt a burst of pain in her gut, and she dreaded she might throw up again. She pushed past the man so she could reach the window. "Excuse me," she shouted, "I'm trying to find someone."

"Of course you are," the man said. "You're the night nurse."

"What?" Tess asked, wondering about his words. Then she remembered her costume.

The man explained, "The night nurse takes care of everyone after dark." He gave a grin and drifted toward the dance floor.

Tess wasn't able to spot James among the throng of people on the deck. Her pain increased, and she clamped her eyes shut. When she opened them again, she noticed there was an insect on the outside of the window. The roach-sized bug was directly in front of her face. She stepped backwards. Despite night's darkness, she could see the insect's crimson coloring and the eyes bulging from either side of its head.

It was a redbug. Tess had watched enough TV news reports to know.

"James…." she whispered. She looked past the insect at the deck, concerned that other bugs might land on those who were outside. But as she searched for her friend, she heard screams sounding from within the club. She turned back toward the crowd and her body tensed up.

She could see the nearby dancing mummy had a few insects on his bandaged back. Tess was about to warn him, but other sights distracted her.

Redbugs swarmed past a violet strobe light.

Three muscular men in Speedos swatted at the insects crawling on their chests and tumbled off a platform into a lake of flesh.

The dance floor mass seethed toward Tess.

Someone grabbed her arm. It was James.

"We need to get out of here now!" he shouted.

People were shrieking as Tess and James squeezed through the exit to the deck. Tess saw patrons fall as they fled, and at one point she thought she felt someone's arm beneath her feet. She spotted a redbug burrowing into a woman's bleeding neck.

"Help me!" the woman cried, and her eyes met Tess's. Before Tess could respond, the throng of fleeing people pinned her and James against a wall. Tess lost her breath when someone elbowed her in the gut.

James pulled her away from the wall. "Look!" he said. He pointed at the banister across the deck from them. The banister was bending from the crowd pressing against it. Tess heard a loud cracking noise as the banister broke.

The crowd spilled over the edge of the deck, and the screaming intensified.

James motioned toward a green *FIRE EXIT* sign above one corner of the deck. "There's another staircase that goes down to the street," he yelled.

Before reaching that staircase, Tess glanced back up at Nightweb and saw hundreds of insects' red bodies resting on the insides of the windows.

"We need to get back to First Hill," Tess said when she realized James was leading her deeper into the industrial section of the city. They'd reached a street lined with warehouses.

James brought her across a dark road and into an even darker alley. He reached inside his doctor's bag and pulled out a lighter and a sweatshirt. He offered the sweatshirt to Tess with a trembling hand.

"Put this on and pull the hood over your head," he said.

"That's not going to keep the bugs away," Tess said, suddenly aware of her renewed sobriety. Fear and adrenaline had overpowered the drug. "We need to get back-"

"Going back to First Hill means going through swarms of bugs," James said. He removed a plastic baggy from beneath the waistband of his scrubs and clicked on the lighter's flame, which showed a number of tablets in the baggy. He selected one and held it out to Tess.

"It'll give us courage," he said.

Tess knocked the tablet out of his hand. "Are you crazy? I don't want to get high again. You should never have drugged me in the first place."

James clicked off the lighter. Despite the darkness, Tess could see him pop a tablet into his mouth. He searched inside his doctor's bag and removed a pack of cigarettes.

Tess remembered her cell phone was inside her purse. She thought she could call the police, or maybe a friend who would pick them up.

After unlocking the phone, she saw on its screen the little blue box that read *1 new message from Mom.*

She tapped on the box and read the following:

Sweet Tess. Bug got under my skin. It's in there still. So sorry. I love you

The phone showed the message had arrived over an hour ago, when Tess was in Nightweb.

Tess felt the tears coming as she stared at her mother's words. "You see?" she said to James, who was having trouble clicking on the flame of the lighter. She held up the phone's screen before him and repeated more loudly, "You see? This is what happens when you're not safe."

The flame finally came, and James held it to the cigarette protruding from between his lips. He looked at Tess with eyes glazed by EZ's effects.

"Is something wrong?" he asked.

Tess was about to scream at him, but the glow of the lighter showed the redbug that had landed on his temple. Tess watched in horror as the insect's wings began to flutter.

MID-FALL

Tess brought her face near one of the watchtower windows to stare up at the fourth floor of Center 6's main building. That was the floor where her mother had been prone and unconscious in bed since arriving at this refugee center for nest people in October. Tess pressed her face against the glass and imagined her mother appearing in the window of her room, 4F, and waving down at her. Tess recalled her mother's wry smile and the way she would sometimes wink at her.

"She'll wake up," Tess whispered to herself. She had vowed to remain a volunteer at Center 6 at least until she could speak with her mother and see in her eyes that she was going to recover.

Tess knew if there was a place where her mother would get better, it would be Center 6. She looked down at the brochures in her hand and read the words on one of the covers:

WELCOME TO A SAFEHAVEN
A Guide to Your Stay
In a United States Refugee Center

She glanced up when she heard the vehicle she was expecting. She moved to the window opposite of the one where she'd been standing. From her new position, she saw the insecticide-spraying wall that bordered Center 6. She also saw the exterminators' camouflaged Humvee ascending the deserted, littered stretch of Westlake Avenue that ran through the No Police Territory and ended at Lake Union. Tess noticed the building that had been burning so brightly by the lake last night was now only producing smoke. She could still see the blackened corpses scattered across the deck of what was once a trendy South Lake Union restaurant.

She hurried down the tower's stairwell and pulled open the heavy gate for the Humvee. There used to be two security guards who'd been in charge of greeting new patients to Center 6. But more and more staff members had quit or disappeared since the redbug swarms had been worsening and word was circulating that Center 6 would be shutting down and transferring its patients to other centers.

Tess stood tall and smiled cheerfully as the Humvee entered the center's driveway. She tried to imagine she was in a floral dress with a Hawaiian lei around her neck, welcoming tourists to some hotel resort on Maui. Why dwell on the reality that she was wearing a Hazard Wrap on a grim, drizzly November day in redbug-infested Seattle, and she was about to speak with people who had insects compromising their cognitive abilities?

One of the exterminators stepped out of the passenger side of the vehicle. He wore the usual exterminator helmet and suit, an outfit that always made Tess think of astronauts. He nodded stiffly at her and opened a rear door.

Another exterminator emerged from the Humvee and motioned for Tess to enter. "We had to get one of the nest people out of the car in Everett," he said in a gruff voice. "We left her in a parking lot. Bug looked like it was going to burst out of her neck, and we couldn't have that thing flying around inside the car."

Tess nodded solemnly, careful to mask her contempt for the exterminator's nonchalance. He clearly lacked compassion for whomever he'd kicked out of the vehicle. Tess had often thought it was unfortunate that all the exterminators had to be men. But she knew Homeland Security's excuse: Female exterminators were at too high a risk. For whatever reason, redbugs attacked them more often than they attacked male exterminators.

Tess stepped inside the Humvee and pulled the door partway shut behind her for some privacy.

There were three rows of seats. The first row was empty. A woman not much older than Tess sat in the second row, staring ahead of her with a vacant gaze. She wore a soiled waitress uniform and had curly blonde hair that looked dusty. On her neck was a purplish patch of inflammation marking where the redbug had entered her.

In the row behind her was a balding, middle-aged man and, clinging to him, a girl who must have been 8 or 9 years old. They both watched Tess with frightened eyes.

Tess held out a brochure for the young woman in the second row. "Welcome to Center 6," she told the passengers. "My name's Tess. I want to assure you you're safe here."

The woman didn't take the brochure. She continued staring ahead of her.

Tess looked at the tag tied around the woman's wrist. It read: *X – Gretchen Wern, Marysville, WA.* Tess was grateful the exterminators had already completed infestation checks on their passengers.

Tess reached out and touched the woman's bare forearm. "Gretchen?" she asked. "Can you tell me your home address?"

"I took out the trash," the woman said, still looking ahead of her. "In back of the diner. I took out the trash. I took out the trash. I took out-"

"Gretchen!" Tess said in a loud voice. She knew she needed to capture the woman's attention. If Gretchen became too excited or anxious she could dislodge the insect from its resting place. When a redbug left the body of a nest person, that person occasionally lived but usually died. The person would suffer the typical symptoms of a redbug victim—profuse sweating, hives breaking out all over the body, convulsions, skin darkening from cell death—but at an accelerated rate.

Tess glanced outside the Humvee and was grateful to see Ahmed, one of the other volunteers, nearing the vehicle.

"She can go to Floor 5," Tess told Ahmed.

Floor 5 held the severely cognitively impaired patients. When she was on the intake shift, Tess made the first suggestion for routing patients. But, of course, Yvette—the Center Coordinator and Dr. Magnison's wife—had the final say. Tess moved to the third row of seats so Ahmed would have a clear path to extract Gretchen from the Humvee. Tess was relieved that Gretchen left the vehicle without a struggle.

Tess looked at the young girl sitting beside her. The girl still held on to the man, who smiled weakly at Tess. Despite the cold air seeping into the vehicle, his forehead was wet with sweat.

Tess noticed the tag dangling from his wrist. The girl didn't have one.

"This is my daughter, Jo," he said. "I'm Stephen Shelton."

"Hello, Jo and Stephen," Tess said. She handed Stephen a brochure. When he opened it, Tess checked his face and neck for an entry wound. She saw a fresh-looking scab beneath one of his thinning tufts of brown hair.

"Stephen," Tess asked, "can you tell me your home address?"

"Don't say anything," Jo immediately warned her father. She glared at Tess. "He's not going in that building. We want the men to take us back home. We were fine in our house."

Stephen slipped an arm around his daughter and hugged her closely. He looked down at her and said, "You know we weren't fine, honey. We were trapped in the basement. We were out of food and almost out of water. I had this-" He was silent as he touched the redbug entry wound on his head.

His eyes met Tess's. "Our home address was 232 Maplewood Lane," he said. "I saw the exterminators from the one window in the basement. They were spraying houses in our neighborhood. It was kind of them to bring us here."

Tess gave him a reassuring smile. "You'll have your own room," she said. "The exterminators will drive Jo to Center 2."

"Can't she stay here with me?" Stephen asked, his grip tightening around his daughter.

"I'm sorry. This center is only for...patients." During her sensitivity training, Tess had learned never to use the term "nest people" when speaking to or around patients.

"You can't take my dad," Jo said, her eyes tearing. "He's staying with me."

"Tess," Ahmed said. He poked his head inside the Humvee. Tess could see his concern through the plastic face shield of his Hazard Wrap.

"We need to get things moving. There are swarms in the area."

Tess nodded. She looked at Stephen. "Please come with me, Mr. Shelton."

"No!" Jo screamed. She collapsed in her father's lap, and her body shook as she wept.

Tess felt her own sadness expand in her chest. She thought of her unconscious mother, and how she'd only been allowed to see her once a week during the seven weeks she'd been volunteering at Center 6. Yvette had explained, "Normally we don't allow any visitors on Floor 4. The insects in those patients are close to exiting. You can see your mother more often if she eventually changes floors."

Tess touched Jo's shoulder. "Sometimes you have to be separate from your family for everyone's good," she said. "You'll see your dad again. This isn't forever. Just until he gets better."

She looked at Stephen. He was nodding, but she could see the doubt in his eyes.

"There's a very capable doctor who runs this center," Tess added with sincerity. "Dr. Magnison. I believe in him. He and other doctors hired by the government are working to find a solution so all families can be together again."

Jo continued to cry.

Tess's voice cracked when she told Stephen, "I'll let you say your goodbyes."

"Come on, sweetie," Stephen whispered to his daughter.

Tess stepped outside the Humvee. The sky was a dark gray, and its clouds tumultuous. Tess saw bits of dead leaves blowing over the wall and into the center's courtyard. She knew redbugs would soon be replacing those leaves. She felt herself sinking into sadness once again, and she glanced up at the fourth floor to try to rise above it.

Someone squeezed her arm.

Ahmed stood next to her and watched her with those handsome chestnut eyes of his. Those eyes often showed an affection for her, but she always tried to stay immune to Ahmed's crush. She did sometimes wonder what it would be like to kiss him.

"Hey," Ahmed said. "I'd much rather stand next to you than them." He nodded in the direction of the two exterminators, who leaned statue-like against the hood of the Humvee. They both stared at the distant wall's insecticide mist with dazed expressions. Tess didn't want to guess what those men had seen on their tour. She'd seen enough in Seattle over the past two months.

"Is the father coming?" Ahmed asked.

"He's coming," she said, sounding deflated. She realized she'd lost her hotel resort persona.

"I have good news for you from Yvette. She said you can see your mom once we take this guy inside."

"What?" Tess smiled widely. "But it's only been four days since my last visit."

Ahmed shrugged. "Maybe Yvette's defrosting, but I doubt it."

"She's been very good to me," Tess said in a defensive voice. "She could have refused to let me volunteer here."

Tess remembered when she'd first asked for the position so she could be closer to her mother.

"You know what will probably happen to her," Yvette had said, peering into her eyes.

"But not necessarily, right?" Tess asked.

"No, I suppose not. And we are in serious need of volunteers. Most of the professionals we'd employ at the center have left the city."

Ahmed placed a hand on Tess's back. "So what do you think about getting a drink with me after you see your mom? We can talk about how it went. I want to talk to you about something else, too."

"I can't do that," Tess said. She thought of James and the night of the club. After they'd finally returned to the apartment, James went into seizures on the living room floor. Tess kept hearing the same recording when she dialed 9-1-1. *All circuits are busy right now. Please hold for the next available operator and be prepared to give the nature of your emergency.*

"I'm sorry," she told Ahmed, "but after I see my mom I should be alone."

She left him and returned to the Humvee. Inside the vehicle, she worked up a smile and said, "Stephen. Jo. It's time."

Tess waited in the hallway outside Stephen Shelton's room, just as Yvette had instructed. Yvette was going to escort her from the sixth floor, where all the highly functional patients stayed, to the fourth floor, which held her mother and the rest of the unconscious patients. When the government converted this building from a cancer research clinic into a refugee center for nest people, it decided to place the highly functional patients on the top floor. They were the most likely to attempt escape.

Tess heard a tapping down the hall. She saw a young woman's pale face peering at her through the wire mesh window of Room 6C. Tess went to the door and read the nametag beneath the window.

"Hello, Rachel," she said. She hadn't seen Rachel since she'd welcomed her to Center 6 about a week ago. Tess sometimes helped the center staff members prep for their visits with the patients, but she rarely interacted with patients after they arrived at the center.

She remembered how Rachel had come in a van driven by an emaciated refugee couple from Spokane. The husband and wife had found her wandering along the side of Interstate 90. When Tess greeted Rachel, the 22-year-old stared out one of the van's windows with both hands over her stomach. She repeated the words, "This is when I need you to be with me, Carlos."

"Will you please open the door for me?" Rachel now asked. She seemed lucid as she stared at Tess with those large hazel eyes. Tess found her pretty despite her wild, unbrushed red hair and the bruise-like smudges beneath her eyes. Her hospital gown matched her hair. Patients on Floor 6 wore red gowns while those on 5 wore pink and those on 4 wore blue.

"I don't have a key," Tess said. "Volunteers aren't allowed to let patients out of their rooms."

"Please," Rachel said. "I'd like some exercise."

Tess tried to utilize her training as a greeter to calm this patient. "Can you take a deep breath?" she asked. "Close your eyes while you breathe and know you're in a safe place."

Rachel narrowed her eyes, but she didn't close them. "There are no safe places anymore," she said.

Tess wasn't sure how to respond. No patient had ever challenged her this way before. Following a pause, she said, "You're safer in your room than you are in the world out there." She motioned toward the window at the end of the hallway.

Her heartbeat quickened when she looked through that window.

Moving over Lake Union toward the city center was a massive, quickly shifting cloud of redbugs. The swarm was so dense it made a shadow on the lake's gray water. Tess had seen many swarms over the past couple months, but none the size of this one.

"What is it?" Rachel asked.

Tess looked at her. "Insects," she said, sounding nervous. She tried to regain her sureness. "But they're out there. We're protected in here."

"I have a bug in my fucking neck. I'm not protected." Rachel turned her head to one side and pressed her neck against the window. Tess saw the scar of her original entry wound, which was just beneath her earlobe. The insect had migrated about five inches down toward her shoulder, where there was a red, swollen bump that was the length of a redbug.

Rachel once again stared at Tess. Her eyes were glassy with tears. "Please," she said. "Isn't there any way you can give me a break from this cell?"

Tess wanted to open the door for her. She remembered Rachel saying on the day of her arrival that the redbugs had killed almost everyone in her family.

"I watched my sister Beth die," Rachel had told her. "And Carlos-"

Tess placed a palm against the wire mesh window. "I'm sorry," she said. "I know you've suffered a lot. I can ask one of the staff to let you out."

Rachel suddenly stepped back from the window and wiped the moisture from her eyes. "I don't trust that doctor."

"Dr. Magnison?" Tess asked. She stepped closer to the door. "But he's a very intelligent man. He's working to find a solution-"

"I don't trust that doctor. I don't trust that doctor. I don't-"

"Tess!" someone called from the end of the hallway.

Tess saw Yvette's willowy figure standing by the door to the stairwell. Tess had guessed Yvette was in her early fifties, but heavy make-up and light plastic surgery made the woman appear a decade younger. Yvette wore her usual pale pink lab coat over a yellow dress that was the same color as her long, bleached hair. She stared at Tess with those violet eyes that always reminded Tess of cat's eyes.

"Why are you talking to her?" Yvette asked in a disapproving voice.

"She wanted me to let her out," Tess said. She glanced through the window and saw that Rachel had retreated to her cot, where she sat with her head in her hands.

"Of course she does," Yvette said. "She's been difficult lately." She motioned for Tess to come with her into the stairwell. The movement of her arm made her gold bracelets jangle.

When Tess neared, Yvette said, "Ignore whatever she told you. She's just moody because she's pregnant."

Tess's eyes widened with surprise. She was about to ask how Center 6 staff treated pregnant patients differently from regular patients, but she was too anxious to see her mother to begin a conversation. She started down the stairs, moving ahead of Yvette.

"Wait," Yvette said. She leaned over the metal railing of the stairwell to stare at one of the blue stained glass window panels. "Do you hear that?"

Tess listened. She thought she heard rain pattering against the window, but she soon realized it was the sound of redbugs hitting glass.

"It's worse than I thought it would be," Yvette said. "We don't have time for you to see your mother."

"Oh, please," Tess said before she could control herself. She blushed at her impudence, but she'd wanted so badly to have the visit.

Yvette looked down at her. Tess thought she saw a flash of sympathy in the woman's eyes.

"I'll let you peek through the window at her," Yvette said. "But then you need to go home. All staff will need to go home before night falls. This could be a bad swarm. They've only been getting worse."

Tess always felt slightly queasy when she approached the door of her mother's room. She'd think of the day she'd finally gone to visit her father in the hospital and found a corpse in his bed. Her father had become this gray-skinned, gaunt-faced thing with its eyes rolled back in its head and its mouth open.

Tess stopped a few feet from the door to her mother's room and allowed Yvette to go before her. "Is she all right?" she asked.

"She's still unconscious."

Tess came to the door and looked through the window. She saw her mother lying in her bed with her head propped up on a couple pillows. She had a large bandage taped beneath her chin and an IV in one wrist. Gray streaks had invaded her mane of dyed red hair. Tess frowned when she saw her mother's eyes were open enough to reveal the whites of her eyeballs.

"You know this center's closing, don't you?" Yvette asked Tess in a solemn voice.

"I've heard," Tess said, glancing from her mother to Yvette. "But you're just moving the center, right? You and Dr. Magnison are still going to take care of the patients, aren't you?"

Yvette looked down at the floor. "We're moving the patients to other centers." Her eyes met Tess's. "I don't think you should be here when we move your mother. It will be too hard for you."

"Will you and Dr. Magnison go to the same center as her? Dr. Magnison's an excellent-"

"Your mother will be in the hands of the government. Dr. Magnison and I are leaving the state. We're going to focus on research. You should leave the area, too. The Northwest is becoming the grim corner of the country."

Tess thought of her two older brothers, who both lived in Phoenix. They'd tried to convince her to join them after the redbugs first appeared in Seattle. But Tess knew she could never abandon her mother.

She felt a headache forming as she imagined trying to volunteer at her mother's next refugee center. She'd had a difficult enough time getting her volunteer position here. She looked back at her mother and asked Yvette, "It's better to be a nest person than to have a bug just land on you, don't you think? That's what I told my brothers. Because if you're a nest person you have a chance at survival. Not all people lose their minds when they have a bug inside them, right?" She looked at Yvette and held her breath as she waited for an answer.

Yvette glanced at the window down the hallway and sighed. There was a flurry of redbugs beyond the glass.

"Not all nest people lose their minds," Yvette said. "Some are like those who've suffered a minor head injury. But most have the cognitive abilities of Alzheimer's patients, or those who've gone through extensive electroshock therapy."

Tess noticed her mother's chest moving with her breath. She asked, "But it's possible that a nest person could have the bug come out of her and she'd be perfectly healthy again, isn't it? I mean both physically and mentally."

"You need to go home now," Yvette said. "For your safety."

"But it is possible, isn't it? For a nest person to fully recuperate?"

"Yes," Yvette said with a hint of irritation. "Unlikely. But I suppose it's possible."

Tess gave her a hug. Yvette's body felt stiff, and the woman didn't embrace her in return.

Yvette started toward the stairwell, the heels of her black shoes clacking on the floor.

"Will you please close my mother's eyes before you leave tonight?" Tess asked.

Yvette didn't look back. She continued toward the stairwell and said, "I think we can manage that."

Tess sat in the rear of the shuttle that delivered center staff members and volunteers home each day. This evening the shuttle only carried Tess and two nurses, both of whom looked down at the aisle with worried expressions on their faces. All passengers wore Hazard Wraps. The air outside Center 6 was still filled with redbugs. As the shuttle exited the center's garage, Tess glanced outside the rear window and spotted Dr. Magnison through one of the first-floor windows.

Flanked by Yvette and a nurse, he perused a patient chart. He was bald except for a shock of white hair on either side of his head. He wore thick, brown glasses and his usual white lab coat. He also sported a hunter orange tie. Tess always appreciated his bright ties and the wide smiles he offered when she passed him in the hallways. Volunteers weren't supposed to talk to Dr. Magnison unless he addressed them first, but Tess guessed the doctor would have a good sense of humor if she spoke with him.

She was surprised to see Dr. Magnison look up from his chart and wave at the departing shuttle. As she waved back, she felt like she was acknowledging her and her mother's guardian.

The sky was nearly dark as the shuttle ascended Westlake Avenue toward downtown. Behind the shuttle was the unlit No Police Territory. Soon after the redbugs had invaded Seattle in late September, the government urged evacuation of the city. The government announced it would focus on securing Seattle's core neighborhoods—downtown, Capitol Hill, First Hill, Pioneer Square, Belltown, and Queen Anne—and the outlying areas would become part of the No Police Territory. Military and exterminator bases and insecticide-spraying walls sprouted in the Secure Territory, while the No Police Territory devolved into areas of robberies, gunshots, fires, and power outages.

Of course, the Secure Territory had its own troubles. Tess often spotted a corpse sprawled on the sidewalk or in a gutter during her evening commute. The government-controlled markets sometimes had bare shelves due to the difficulty in transporting foods and products. There were occasionally rolling blackouts in the core neighborhoods.

Tess noticed the Space Needle was without light tonight.

As the shuttle crossed the freeway overpass toward First Hill, it drove by an abandoned light rail train. Tess looked at the dark windows of that train and wondered what James's family had done with his body. Tess had tried phoning him after the hospital discharged him, but he never answered. One morning Tess saw his name on a list of redbug victims printed in *The Seattle Times.*

"Tess?"

Tess stopped gazing out the window and realized the driver was waiting for her to leave the vehicle.

"This is your stop, honey."

"Thanks, Hank," Tess called to the driver. The rear door opened and the tiny nozzles adorning the doorframe sprayed their insecticide mist. Tess ran through that mist toward her and her mother's apartment building. She was grateful not to feel any insects collide with her. She guessed the massive swarm was staying downtown for now.

Before reaching the doorway, she glanced up at the 15-story apartment building. Few of the windows were lit. Tess predicted the building would soon be vacant. After the establishment of the Secure Territory, the government had given residents Anti-Redbug Kits on a weekly basis. But the deliveries had become less frequent as the swarms increased.

In the apartment building's lobby, Tess noticed the plastic bottle of insecticide spray on top of the mailboxes was nearly empty of its green liquid. The handwritten sign reading *MAKE SURE YOU'RE BUG FREE* had fallen from the wall to the tiled floor.

She saw someone had recently entered the building. There was a sprinkling of orange flower petals in the lobby.

When she left the elevator on the 9th floor, Tess recognized the building's most recent visitor. Ahmed stood outside the door of her and her mother's apartment. He wore a Hazard Wrap, but he'd pulled off the portion that protected his head. He held a bouquet of dried orange flowers.

"What are you doing here?" Tess asked. Part of her was pleased to see him outside her home, but the other, anxious part of her recalled James's fateful visit.

"I really wanted to talk to you," Ahmed said as Tess unlocked the door. "I also wanted to give you these." He held out the bouquet for her, causing more petals to drop.

"Sorry if I'm making a mess," he said. "These are the best flowers I could find."

Tess received the bouquet with an awkward smile and a flushed face. She led him inside the dark apartment and quickly moved to click on the lamp near the couch. She set the bouquet on the coffee table. "You really shouldn't be going around the city tonight," she said. "There's a storm of bugs out there."

She neared the windows to make sure no insects had broken the glass. She regularly sprayed the windows with the sealant the government had provided residents, but she was always nervous the insects would overpower it. She pulled the curtains shut so the windows would give off less light.

"I wanted to talk to you about something Dr. Magnison has," Ahmed said. "Something he's hiding."

Tess began removing her Hazard Wrap. She hoped this wouldn't give Ahmed the signal that he should stay. "And what would that be?" she asked in a dubious voice. She was becoming weary of Ahmed criticizing Dr. Magnison and Yvette. They were icy people, he'd said. They were too clinical with the patients. They wore designer ties and dresses around people who'd lost everything. They were always having conference calls with pharmaceutical reps.

"Dr. Magnison has what could be the antidote," Ahmed said.

"The antidote?" Tess asked. She stopped unzipping her protective top.

"To redbug toxin."

Tess's surprise kept her from speaking.

"I overheard him talking to Yvette about it. Remember the girl the exterminators found in the mountains a couple weeks ago?"

Tess nodded. The girl had had long, braided black hair and a hippie-ish name. The name of a season or a flower. She was severely cognitively impaired, and she could only make a biting motion when she tried to speak. She died within days of her arrival.

"Remember that big duffel bag the girl was carrying?" Ahmed asked. "Inside that bag was a gallon-sized milk container holding this gooey yellow stuff. I saw the container in Yvette's office when I brought her a latte."

"And how would anyone know it's an antidote?" Tess asked.

"There was also a note in that duffel bag," Ahmed said, "signed by a bunch of naturopaths. The note said the gooey stuff was a potential antidote and included application instructions. I heard Dr. Magnison and Yvette talking about it yesterday. I heard them through the door of Yvette's office."

Tess started to smile. "But this is wonderful," she said. She imagined her mother opening her eyes and whispering, "I'm all right, Tess. Everything's going to be all right."

"No," Ahmed said. "It's not wonderful. Because Dr. Magnison and Yvette aren't going to do anything with it until they move out of state. They're planning on getting funding for research studies with the stuff. Just think how many people are going to die in the meantime."

Tess remembered Yvette saying she and Dr. Magnison were going to focus on research. But she couldn't imagine them depriving anyone of an antidote that actually worked. They were professionals in the medical industry, and the government had granted them their high-level positions at Center 6.

"I can't believe they wouldn't act sooner than that," Tess told Ahmed, shaking her head. She finished removing her Hazard Wrap. "We can ask them about their plans. Yvette would tell me. She's been kind to me."

"She's a spider," Ahmed said in a raised voice. "One day you'll finally recognize that. But I didn't come here to debate about her and Dr. Magnison. I came to say I'm going to take that antidote and make sure someone puts it to good use. And I need you to help me take it."

"You're going to steal it?" Tess asked.

"Not steal. Just get it to the right person. I know this nurse at Center 3 I really trust."

"I trust Dr. Magnison," Tess said. "And Yvette. My mother's in their care, and-"

"Are you going to help me or not? I just need you to keep an eye on the hallway outside Yvette's office."

"No." Tess stood on the other side of the couch from Ahmed. She placed her hands on her hips. "The patients at Center 6 could benefit from that antidote. My mother could benefit from it."

"It's not for nest people. It's for healthy people—like you and me—to prevent us from dying if a bug lands on us."

"How do you know it can't help a nest person?" Tess asked, her face reddening with anger. "You're not a doctor."

"You trust anyone in a lab coat, don't you?" Ahmed asked.

"I trust my mother's doctor," Tess said, her hands forming fists.

"Grow up, Tess. You've got to act like an adult while the world is turning to rot. I know it's hard, but you should realize your mother won't be around for long."

"Get out!" Tess yelled. "I never asked you to come over here." She picked up the bouquet of flowers from the coffee table and threw them at Ahmed's chest. The bouquet exploded all over her mother's Persian entry rug.

Ahmed backed up toward the front door. His handsome eyes gave a look of regret. "Tess," he said in a tender voice.

Tess came around the couch and stomped toward him. "Get the fuck out!" she screamed.

Ahmed opened the door and retreated down the hallway. He pressed the button to summon the elevator. The doors immediately opened.

"Please don't say anything," he told Tess, who now stood in the doorway with her arms folded over her chest.

"I don't want you talking to me at work unless you have to," Tess said. "Do you hear me? We're not friends or anything. We're just co-workers."

Ahmed nodded before stepping inside the elevator. The doors shut.

Tess collapsed against the doorframe and sighed. Oddly, she felt more relief than disappointment. She was thankful Ahmed would no longer complicate her life with his flirtatiousness or his rebellious plans. She was also thankful there existed a substance that might help so many, and possibly her mother.

She was relishing this thought when she noticed her neighbor's door was open a crack.

Francisca was a 47-year-old Pilates instructor who'd refused to leave the city when the bugs arrived. She'd told Tess she'd escaped a physically abusive husband in Sao Paulo and a devoutly religious family that regularly mourned her choice not to become a mother.

"If I can get away from all that and start my own Pilates studio in America," Francisca had said, "then I'm certainly not going to freak out about some poisonous cockroaches."

Tess gently pushed open the door and peered into the dim interior of Francisca's apartment. "Hello?" she asked.

The apartment smelled of Francisca's spicy tomato sauce. Francisca sometimes gave Tess meatballs drenched in the sauce for her lunches at Center 6.

"Francisca, are you home?" Tess called. She noticed the only light in the apartment came from above the kitchen island. Sitting on that island was a pot filled with the tomato sauce. Next to the pot was an overturned bowl that had produced a splatter of red liquid.

"Francisca!" Tess shouted, sounding more panicked. She looked in the direction of Francisca's bedroom, and that was when she noticed the blanketed figure on the couch. She moved from the doorway to the dim living room. As she stood over the couch, she realized nobody lay on its cushions. There were only rumpled blankets—a patterned quilt, a polyester blanket, and a white sheet.

Tess remembered Francisca saying she always slept on the couch because she hated hearing the redbugs' legs tapping against her bedroom window.

Tess heard a tapping now, coming from behind her.

She turned back toward the kitchen and saw a redbug repeatedly flying into the light above the kitchen island.

She also saw a person sitting against the wall past the opened front door. The charred-looking figure only wore pink panties and a green T-shirt with the words *BRASIL * BRAZIL* across the front. Tess recognized that the corpse was Francisca's.

She screamed.

Her screaming grew louder when the redbug flew in her direction.

Tess ducked to avoid the insect and yanked the white sheet off the couch. She fell onto the floor and covered herself with the sheet. The redbug landed on the fabric near her face. This insect was thicker than others she'd seen, and the hook-like claws at the ends of its front legs appeared especially sharp.

"No no no," Tess cried. She thought of how she needed to stay alive for her mother, and the thought gave her enough courage to push out on the sheet and trap the redbug in its folds. She threw the material to the floor and stamped on it with her shoe until she saw the yellow smear of the smashed insect.

Before leaving the apartment, Tess covered Francisca with the quilt and turned out the light above the kitchen island. She then returned to her and her mother's apartment to pack her suitcase.

She wasn't going to wait for the redbugs to invade the entire building. She would move into Center 6 and be near her mother. And when her mother moved to a new center, she would follow her.

Tess arrived at Center 6's front gate just before sunrise. She usually showed up by shuttle at 9, but this morning she'd had one of the government-subsidized taxis take her. She'd spent a final night in her and her mother's apartment. She wedged a towel into the crack beneath her bedroom door. Just in case a redbug crawled past that barrier, she slept in a Hazard Wrap.

She now set down her suitcase on the weedy sidewalk and glanced at the uppermost window of the center's watchtower. A fluorescent light glowed inside, helping to distinguish the tower from the charcoal-gray sky. No figure peered out the window to watch for approaching exterminators or an unexpected visitor like Tess. A volunteer or staff member was supposed to man that tower from 7 a.m. to 7 p.m. every day. Tess couldn't remember who was scheduled to volunteer this morning. She was the only one who consistently came each day of the week.

"You can go," she told the taxi driver. "They'll let me in. I work here."

The driver nodded, and the taxi immediately sped away. Tess looked toward the sky again. She was grateful the bug storm had passed. She hadn't seen a single insect make contact with the taxi's windshield during the drive to Center 6.

She heard the sound of approaching vehicles, and she turned to see two of the center's shuttles coming from downtown. The first stopped outside the gate and opened its doors for her.

Tess carried her suitcase on board through the mist of insecticide spray. She recognized the driver as one of the exterminators who'd dropped off the three patients yesterday. His partner sat in the seat directly behind him. Both men wore exterminator suits. The only other passenger on the shuttle was Yvette, who sat in the far back. She wore a Hazard Wrap, and Tess could see she was frowning.

"What are you doing here?" Yvette asked. "I texted you and told you to take the day off."

"I rarely check my phone anymore," Tess said. Her mother used to call her more than anyone else.

The driver honked the horn, startling Tess. She realized he was signaling for someone to open the gate. She walked along the aisle and sat near Yvette, who had puffy, tired-looking eyes.

"Who was on the early morning shift?" Tess asked.

"Ahmed was supposed to be."

Tess raised her eyebrows.

"What's that look for?" Yvette asked.

Tess wasn't ready to betray Ahmed and mention the antidote. After all, he'd only talked about taking the substance. He hadn't actually stolen it yet. She looked through the rear window at the second shuttle. She couldn't tell who was in that vehicle.

"Why are the shuttles out so early?" she asked. "And why's an exterminator driving?"

"Government business," Yvette said, sounding defensive. "Which means it's none of your business."

Tess gave her a wounded look, and Yvette shook her head.

"I apologize for my tone," Yvette said. "I barely slept last night. Now why don't you tell me why you're here so early."

"I can't be home anymore," Tess said as the shuttle drove into the center's courtyard. "There are bugs in the building. I want to stay at the center so I can be close to my mom." She almost asked Yvette why she didn't want her to come to the center today, but she decided not to risk irritating the woman further.

"You know the center's closing," Yvette said, "and it looks like that'll happen sooner rather than later. Probably in the next few days."

"I'll just stay until my mom goes."

"I told you I don't want you here when that happens," Yvette said, her voice cracking.

Tess thought she saw tears in Yvette's eyes.

But then Yvette's look turned steely and she said, "You can stay here for the night. We'll take you to a hotel tomorrow."

"And you'll tell me when my mom moves, and where she goes, right?"

"That's the government's responsibility. Not mine." Yvette shot up from her seat and walked to the doorway while the shuttle was still moving.

Tess went to stand behind her as the vehicle parked in the garage. The second shuttle pulled up alongside their vehicle, and Tess gasped when she saw the second shuttle's doors open.

"Dr. Magnison went, too," she said. She'd never seen Dr. Magnison leave Center 6. She watched him descend the shuttle's steps behind two nurses who rarely worked at the center. One of the nurses appeared to be crying, and Dr. Magnison was speaking to her in a firm voice.

"I'll ask that you try to keep a distance from us today," Yvette told Tess. "We're very busy and short-staffed, as you know. We've moved all the patients from Floor 5 to another center."

The shuttles' passengers headed inside Center 6 after a nurse sprayed them with one of the garage's insecticide hoses. Tess noticed that everyone was oddly quiet. She watched Dr. Magnison wander down a corridor with the two nurses who had been in his shuttle. The exterminators went outside the building's main entrance to return to their Humvee, which was parked in the drive. Tess remained in the main hallway with Yvette and Kristen, one of the lead nurses. Yvette had removed her Hazard Wrap while Tess still wore hers. Tess was about to slink away toward the watchtower when she heard Yvette address Kristen.

"Why wasn't Ahmed watching for us? He should have been in the watchtower."

"He says he's ill," Kristen said, scowling. Although she was in her thirties, she had the frown lines of someone much older. "I heard the honking outside, and I came down here and found him standing near the entrance. He told me he felt feverish, and I brought him into the examining room. I didn't see any sign of illness." She pointed down the hall. "He's in there now, and he says he wants to talk to you."

Yvette gave an exasperated sigh. "We really don't have time for this." She started toward the examining room, and Kristen trailed behind her.

Tess watched them pass Yvette's office, and her suspicion grew from a bud to a bloom. After Yvette and Kirsten entered the examining room, she set her suitcase on the hallway floor and tried opening the door to Yvette's office.

Someone had unlocked it.

Tess gently pushed the door open a crack, and she thought she glimpsed movement inside the office. The only light in the room came through the blue frosted window that was opposite the doorway. Tess opened the door further and saw the contents of the office: a disordered desk against one wall, a bookcase and filing cabinets lining the other wall, and, in the center, a large metal table holding clear bags of syringes, boxes of bandages, and the circular plastic containers center staff used for storing biological specimens.

Tess saw someone's hand beneath that table. When she opened the door all the way, the hand withdrew into shadow.

"Who's under there?" Tess asked in an anxious voice.

No one answered.

Tess flipped on the light switch. She moved near the side of the table to see whoever was hiding from her. As she bent over, she spotted a transparent, gallon-sized container holding a yellow substance.

The table suddenly rose up and smashed into her.

Tess fell back onto Yvette's desk and knocked her head against a hand sanitizer dispenser. The table fell onto its side with a crashing noise.

As Tess touched the back of her aching head, Rachel emerged from behind the table. She no longer wore her red Floor 6 hospital gown. She had on the green hooded sweatshirt and black pants she'd worn when she first arrived at the center. She ran out of the office with her long, crimson hair streaming behind her.

She carried the container.

"Wait!" Tess called. She quickly sidestepped around the fallen table and reached the doorway. Rachel stood in the hallway, looking in the direction of the examining room.

Tess noticed Ahmed, Yvette, and Kristen standing outside the examining room. She figured they must have come into the hallway after hearing the sound of the table hitting the floor. Ahmed looked frightened while the other two appeared confused.

"I'm sorry," Rachel called in their direction. Tess realized she was addressing Ahmed.

Rachel slowly set the container on the floor of the hallway. "I got it for you like you asked," she said, "but I guess this didn't work out the way you thought it would, it would, it would, it would-"

Rachel blinked rapidly and looked as if she were trying to escape her thought pattern. She turned and fled toward the main entrance.

"Come back!" Yvette shouted. "You're not allowed to leave."

Tess stepped into the hallway. "I'll get her," she said. She was grateful to see Yvette nod in approval. She avoided looking Ahmed in the eyes.

Tess realized Rachel had a clear route out of Center 6. The gate was still open, and the exterminators' Humvee was gone from the courtyard. As Tess chased after her, she glimpsed Rachel's exposed neck. She wondered whether a nest person was vulnerable to the redbugs. Yvette had said nest people became immune to the insects' toxin and were no longer in danger when they were around redbugs, but Tess had heard a nurse talking about a patient who'd arrived at the center with three insects lodged beneath the back of his skull.

"You're being foolish," Tess called to Rachel, who was clearly a faster runner than her. The protective material covering Tess's head intensified the sound of her labored breathing. She used to jog at Washington State University to help her anxiety, but she'd stopped after moving back to the city to live with her mother.

"We can't help you if you're out here," she called as the pursuit took the women alongside the center's insecticide-spraying wall.

Rachel glanced behind her and shouted, "Just leave me alone!" Once they were past the wall, she veered off the sidewalk and ran across the street. She hurdled a guardrail and headed down a steep hill leading to the No Police Territory.

Tess clumsily followed through waist-high brown grass and scraggly shrubbery. Tess's pace slowed even more as she tried to be careful about not ripping her Hazard Wrap. She would have retreated to Center 6, but she thought of how much Yvette would appreciate her retrieving an escaped patient. She also imagined her mother one day deliriously wandering away from a refugee center. Tess would want someone to guide her back to safety.

After all, nest people needed healthy people to watch over them.

Tess saw Rachel climbing the chain link fence at the bottom of the hill. The fence marked the end of the Secure Territory.

"Stop!" Tess cried. "You don't know what you're getting into over there."

Rachel gave her a resentful scowl and continued over the top of the fence. She jumped down onto a sidewalk littered with broken malt liquor bottles and sprinted across the street toward an office building with smashed windows and graffiti-laden doorways.

Tess climbed the fence. She was grateful someone had cut away a length of the barbed wire that ran along the top of the fence, but she was hesitant about venturing into the No Police Territory.

Rather than descend from the fence, she looked along the street in the direction of Lake Union and saw that all the buildings had been vandalized. Some showed signs of past fires. Weeds and wildflowers had invaded the sidewalks, and ivy vines had climbed telephone poles. Two abandoned vans remained in the intersection where they had once collided.

Tess saw a dumpster about 20 feet along the sidewalk from her. A woman's shriveled corpse sat against the side of that dumpster. The woman had no eyeballs, just empty eye sockets.

Tess felt nauseous. She glanced up at the hillside, hoping she'd spot Center 6's watchtower. She only saw the brown grass trembling in a cold breeze.

Then she noticed a dark red cloud, which she soon recognized to be a swarm of redbugs.

The insects were flying over the street where Tess had run after Rachel. They darted downwards out of view, and then they reappeared over a row of bushes at the top of the hill.

They were flying in Tess's direction.

Tess dropped from the fence into the No Police Territory. Frantic, she glanced up and down the street, wondering where she could find shelter from the swarm. She considering entering one of those crashed vans, but what if dead bodies awaited her inside?

"Over here!"

Tess looked across the street and saw Rachel standing just beyond the remains of a window.

"Hurry, hurry, hurry, hurry," Rachel said, blinking again.

"Stay calm," Tess said as she ran across the street. She was concerned that if Rachel became overexcited the redbug might emerge from her entry wound.

Tess glanced behind her and saw the redbugs pouring through the chain link fence.

"Hurry, hurry, hurry," Rachel continued, taking Tess's hand and helping her over the jagged glass lining the bottom of the window frame.

Despite the lack of light, Tess was able to see they were in the lobby of a corporate office building. In front of them was a large, curving reception desk covered in stumps of melted candles, crushed beer cans, and candy bar wrappers. To the right of the desk was an elevator bank. Tess thought she saw a body lying before one set of elevator doors. She didn't have time to look more closely because Rachel pulled her deeper into the darkness.

"This door should take us into the stairwell," Rachel said. She moved her hand around the face of the door until she reached the handle. The door swung open, and Rachel led them into utter blackness.

Once the door closed, Tess heard aluminum cans rattling in the lobby. She figured the swarm must have entered the space. The sound soon stopped, however, and was replaced by Tess and Rachel's rapid breathing.

"Thank you for helping me," Tess said in a quiet voice.

Rachel replied, "Now will you leave me alone?"

"I'm trying to watch out for you—and your baby. You shouldn't be wandering around the No Police Territory."

"I'm—we're—at greater risk in that center. Dr. Magnison tried to abort my baby."

"What?" Tess wished she could look in Rachel's eyes at the moment. She was certain she'd detect that Rachel was lying. She recalled Ahmed's suspicion of Dr. Magnison, and she wondered if he'd helped turn Rachel against the doctor. After all, he'd convinced her to help him steal the antidote.

"If Ahmed told you that," Tess said, "he-"

"Dr. Magnison told me. He gave me a couple pills and said they would make the pregnancy 'go away.' He told me now wasn't the time to have a child."

Tess failed to explain away this story. She sensed Rachel was speaking the truth. "Did Yvette know about this?" she asked in a timid voice.

"Yvette was in the room. She held the cup of water I was supposed to drink with the pills."

Tess was quiet. She felt as if the darkness of the stairwell was seeping into her.

"I won't give up this baby," Rachel said. "This is Carlos's and my baby."

"Was Carlos your husband?" Tess asked.

"We didn't have enough time for him to become that. He was an exterminator who left his team to take care of my sister Beth and me. Beth and I both had bugs in us. Then the bug came out of Beth one morning and flew onto Carlos."

Rachel choked up. She sounded defeated. "Carlos and I were in bed together when the bug landed on the back of his leg. He died a day later."

Tess reached out to give Rachel a comforting pat on the shoulder, but her fingers touched something sticky. She quickly withdrew her hand, and then she cautiously moved it back to press against what felt like a mound of Jell-O.

"Oh, no," she whispered.

"What is it?" Rachel asked.

Tess reached inside the chest pocket of her Hazard Wrap for her mini-flashlight. She clicked it on, and both Rachel and she flinched.

The walls of the stairwell were covered in redbug nests.

Revolted, Tess stepped backwards. She had only seen a couple of the orange nest networks before. One had coated a brick wall of an alley in Belltown, another had enmeshed with the hanging branches of a willow tree in Freeway Park. The egg sacs in this nest were larger than the others she'd seen.

And she saw movement inside some of the sacs. Little, worm-like bodies protruded from many of the eggs.

Redbugs were in the process of hatching.

Tess noticed Rachel was shielding her stomach with her arms. "Let's go," Tess said, starting toward the door.

"Wait," Rachel whispered. "Look up there." She pointed at the sloping underside of the staircase.

Tess held up the flashlight. She saw about a dozen full-sized redbugs resting on cement, their crimson exoskeletons glimmering in the light from the flashlight. The insects appeared to be watching the two women. Only their feelers moved.

"Why aren't they coming at us?" Rachel asked.

Tess shook her head and moved closer to the door. "Who cares?" She took hold of Rachel's arm and tugged her toward the lobby.

Outside the building, the gray morning sky was free of insects. Tess and Rachel walked together to the middle of the street.

Tess motioned in the direction of downtown's skyscrapers. "You should at least stay in the Secure Territory if you won't go back to Center 6. You'll need to see a doctor."

"And that doctor will just send my baby and me back to a refugee center." Rachel glanced down the street toward the smashed vans. "I'll have to take my chances here. Maybe I'll meet some other nest people. Other nest people. Other nest-"

"Rachel," Tess said, touching her arm. She gave Rachel a worried look.

"Animals give birth on their own," Rachel said, "so why shouldn't we be able to?" She smiled at Tess for the first time.

"You go on back to Center 6 and tell them I outran you and disappeared. That's what could have happened."

"I'll tell them that," Tess said with a weak grin. She felt an ache of sadness in her chest.

Rachel started down the street, but Tess remained in place, watching her.

Rachel looked back. "I'll be fine," she said. "Really, really, really I will."

Tess didn't believe her.

When Tess returned to Center 6, she found the gate was open. A black Humvee waited in the courtyard with its engine running. One exterminator sat in the driver's seat and another spoke with Yvette outside the vehicle. Both exterminators wore their helmets and uniforms while Yvette had on a Hazard Wrap.

Tess didn't recognize either of the men. The one speaking to Yvette had a red, hard-looking face with deep lines under his eyes.

Yvette appeared to stiffen as Tess approached. She gave Tess a desperate look and asked, "Where is she?"

"I lost her." Tess felt as if the exterminator with the red face were studying her.

Yvette flashed him a knowing look and then asked Tess, "Where exactly did you lose her?"

Tess saw the exterminator's eyes were on her again. She didn't want those eyes to ever be on Rachel. "She disappeared a few blocks away from here," she said, "in the Secure Territory. I think she was headed toward downtown."

The exterminator nodded at Yvette and entered the Humvee. The vehicle rolled out of the courtyard.

Yvette patted Tess's back as they entered the center. "I appreciate you trying," she said.

The women stood in the insecticide spray zone between the main entrance's two sets of doors. Those entering the building were required to wait in the spray for 30 seconds. Tess saw through the greenish mist that Yvette was watching her with an odd, almost guilty expression on her face.

"I found a hotel for you," Yvette said. "We're going to pay for your room for the next week. We could have a shuttle take you there this afternoon."

"You said I could stay here tonight," Tess said. "I want to see my mom." She and Yvette left the spray and entered the main hallway, where they began removing their Hazard Wraps.

Yvette's eyes didn't meet Tess's when she said, "I'm afraid you can't see your mom. Floor 4 is on lockdown. A bug came out of one of the patients and we're still trying to find it."

"I can help you," Tess said. "You said you're short-staffed."

"No," Yvette said a little too quickly. Tess suspected she was hiding something.

"We have just enough nurses here," Yvette continued. "You're not trained to deal with that type of a situation."

Tess nodded without agreeing. If Yvette was so concerned about her exposure to redbugs, why did she allow her to chase Rachel outside the center?

"Listen," Yvette said. "You've been a tremendous help. You've worked more hours than a volunteer ever should, and you've done an amazing job greeting new patients. But it's time for you to leave your position."

Tess tried not to let Yvette's compliments sway her. "Where's Ahmed?" she asked.

"We sent him away. The government will see that he's penalized. He put our lives at risk by letting that girl out of her room."

Tess hoped Ahmed wouldn't be punished too severely. After all, his intentions had been altruistic. "What's your plan for the antidote?" she asked.

"Antidote?" Yvette said with raised eyebrows.

"Ahmed told me about what was in that container. I told him you and Dr. Magnison would know what to do with it."

"Of course we do," Yvette said.

"So when will you start giving it to people?"

Yvette laughed and shook her head. "Give it to people?" she asked. "How far do you think a gallon of that will go, my dear? We don't even know if it works. We'll have to do a Phase I trial—and possibly animal studies before that. We'll need to figure out how to reproduce it. And, of course, there's the issue of a patent."

"A patent?" Tess asked, frowning. "But that'll take-"

"Yvette." Dr. Magnison had opened the door to Yvette's office. He motioned for her to come inside. "I've got InfiniPharma on the line."

Yvette looked at Tess. She said, "If you really want to be here today you can stay in the watchtower. I'll have Kristen bring you dinner."

Tess felt herself diminishing in presence and power. She forced a smile when she noticed Dr. Magnison was grinning at her.

"You're a good girl," he said to her after Yvette entered the office. "I appreciate your efforts today. Truly, I do."

Tess wanted to ask Dr. Magnison about his attempt to end Rachel's pregnancy, but she feared she'd sound stupid questioning his medical expertise. She remembered the time he'd harshly lectured one of the nurses on the locations of entry wounds in nest people.

Tess was about to offer a simple "You're welcome," but Dr. Magnison pulled the door shut.

✳

Weirdly, all of Floor 4's windows were dark. Tess stared at the floor from the watchtower, trying to distinguish her mother's window from the others. She told herself maybe the staff had located the stray bug, and Yvette ordered an early lights out for the patients. Tess guessed that even though they were all unconscious, the patients could still be traumatized by the search for the insect. She wished she could sit by her mother's bed and hold her hand.

She turned to look in the direction of the No Police Territory. She was concerned by the row of fires along the shore of Lake Union. It appeared that houseboats were burning. She hoped Rachel had changed her mind and snuck back into the Secure Territory.

Someone climbed the stairs of the watchtower. Tess leaned over the railing to see the figure wore a Hazard Wrap. As the person approached, Tess recognized Kristen's frown lines beyond the face shield.

Kristen looked up at Tess with bleary eyes. "It's almost 11 o'clock," she said. "Yvette wants you to hit the hay. She's prepared a room for you on Floor 5."

"I'd like to see my mom before I go to bed," Tess said.

Kristen shook her head. "Floor 4 is on lockdown," she said in a distant voice.

"Why are all the lights off in the patients' rooms then?" Tess asked.

"I don't run this center. I'm just a nurse. Yvette said you need to get up at 5 a.m. A taxi's going to take you to a hotel. She said she won't be able to see you because we'll be busy transferring Floor 6 patients to another center."

Once the women were back in the main building, Tess followed Kristen up the stairwell. When they reached the landing of her mother's floor, Tess tried looking through the window to the floor's hallway. A metal covering blocked the glass.

After Kristen unlocked the door to Floor 5 with a keycard, Tess noticed that she dropped that keycard in the right pocket of her lab coat.

Kristen brought Tess to a room that had formerly housed a patient. The chamber was now empty except for Tess's suitcase and a cot supporting a stack of folded, fresh sheets.

"I'm spending the night, too," Kristen said in a tired voice, "for the early-morning patient transfer. I'll be in the room next to yours."

Tess nodded and watched her leave the room. Tess was relieved she didn't lock the door.

The tapping continued on the other side of the wall. Tess rolled onto her side and saw the wall was gone and her father lay in a cot beside hers. His face seemed tan, and his shoulder-length brown and gray hair had a moonlit gloss to it. He smiled at her and watched her with loving eyes.

Tess winced in fear when she saw his arm slip out from beneath a blanket. It was a skeleton's arm with bits of flesh still attached to it.

"That wasn't me knocking," he told his daughter in a tender voice. "That was your mother. She's leaving you now."

He pointed across the room with his bony hand. Tess looked toward the window and saw her mother's shadowy figure suspended in the air outside. Her blue hospital gown billowed in the wind.

Tess couldn't see her mother's face. As Tess rose to approach her, the figure floated upwards out of view.

"Wait!" Tess cried.

She opened her eyes and saw she still lay on her cot. The window across the room was concealed by blinds, and a wall was where her father had been. A digital clock on that wall showed the time as *4:24 A.M.*

The tapping began again.

Tess went to the window and opened the blinds. Redbugs speckled the outer surface of the glass. She heard her father's words: *She's leaving you now.*

Tess walked from her room into the dark hallway. She peered through the mesh-wire window of Kristen's chamber. She recognized the nurse's sleeping figure on the cot. She was grateful to also see Kristen's lab coat draped over a swivel chair.

As Tess pulled the keycard out of the coat, she wondered what would happen if a staff member caught her on her mother's floor. Would Yvette compare her to Ahmed and claim she'd endangered others in the building? Tess didn't care. She just needed to see her mother once more.

She tiptoed along the hallway until she reached the stairwell, which was quiet and dimly lit. She listened for others for a few moments, and then she descended the stairs to the landing of Floor 4. She held her breath as she placed the keycard against the sensor on the doorframe.

A green light blinked at the top of the sensor.

Tess opened the door and slipped into the hallway, which was completely dark except for the moonlight coming through the window at the end of the corridor. She ran her hand over the wall by the door until she found a switch.

The lights came on, showing that all the doors along the hallway were ajar.

Tess felt the hammering of her heart as she hurried to her mother's room and pushed the door all the way open.

Tess whimpered, and tears soon stung her eyes.

Her mother's room was empty.

Tess kept screaming "Where is she?" until Yvette entered the hallway.

Accompanying her were the two exterminators Tess had seen the day before. Both men wore exterminator suits and wielded extermination hoses. The one with the red face shadowed Yvette. The other, who'd been in the driver's seat of the black Humvee yesterday, stayed near the door to the stairwell. He had sickly pale skin and purplish circles around his eyes.

The red-faced exterminator glared at Tess and asked, "Is she one now?"

"No," Yvette said in irritated voice. "She's a volunteer. Why don't you two go upstairs and get the patients ready. I'll join you soon."

Tess wiped her eyes as the men returned to the stairwell.

Before closing the door, the pale one asked, "Force if necessary, right?"

Yvette shot him an exasperated look. "If necessary," she said. She then looked at Tess with a hint of remorse.

Tess dried her running nose with the back of a hand and demanded, "Where's my mom?"

Yvette stared into her eyes for some moments. The look was searching, almost interrogating, and it sent a chill rising through Tess's spine.

Yvette folded her arms over her chest. "Yesterday we took your mother and the other patients on this floor to Center 7. That was a government order."

Tess recalled the two shuttles returning to Center 6 before sunrise. "But why didn't you tell me?" she asked. "You said you'd moved patients from Floor 5, not Floor 4."

Yvette hesitated before saying, "I wasn't ready to break the news. You showed up at the center unexpectedly. I'd barely slept. We had to prep for today's move. I was going to tell you this morning, before you left for the hotel."

Tess peered into Yvette's eyes. She thought she'd detected a lie among the woman's words, but she only cared about her mother's location.

"Center 7's all the way down in Tacoma, isn't it?" she asked.

"Yes," Yvette said. Her eyes showed a flicker of nervousness. "But don't go there for a couple days. They're processing your mom. It can take some time for them to complete the screening assessments. Also, it's possible they won't be allowing visitors. The government has been changing some rules."

Tess was about to tell Yvette she wasn't sure she believed her mother was in Center 7, but Dr. Magnison spoke before she could.

"There's my girl."

Dr. Magnison stood in the doorway to the stairwell. Like his wife, he wore a Hazard Wrap. He grinned widely at Tess. "She can come with us in one of the shuttles," he told Yvette. "We could use her help with the patients."

"No, Frank."

Tess had never heard Yvette refer to Dr. Magnison by his first name.

"She's not...in the right state of mind," Yvette said. "I'm going to get her to a hotel."

"We're once again down a nurse," Dr. Magnison told her. "Vanya didn't show. There's just me, you, four exterminators, and Kristen. She could stay in her shuttle-"

"Are you going to Center 7?" Tess asked in an eager voice. She knew she needed to maintain the trust of the Magnisons. Their trust could affect her ability to be with her mother in Center 7 on a regular basis. And she might want to contact Dr. Magnison one day and ask for guidance on her mother's healthcare. "I could help you. How am I going to be of any use in a hotel room?"

"We're going to a new center," Yvette said, her eyes still on her husband. "I don't think-"

"Let the girl come," Dr. Magnison said, glowering at his wife. "I said she can stay in the shuttle." He grinned once more at Tess. "You really do want to help, don't you?"

Tess smiled brightly for the doctor. "I do."

Floor 6 had enough rooms to house 20 patients, but only 17 nest people would be riding the shuttles this morning. Two patients had died last week, and Rachel had traded her space in the refugee center for the streets of the No Police Territory.

As the exterminators directed patients into a queue in the hallway, Tess realized how much these people had changed since they'd arrived at Center 6.

The pretty forty-something woman from Issaquah looked as if she'd torn clumps of hair out of her scalp. The plump woman who'd worked in a grocery store downtown was now bone-thin, and the bug under the skin of her chin had swollen to a gruesome size, as if it had been feeding on her excess weight. The once hopeful-looking teenage boy who'd found his own way to the center now stared ahead of him with dim eyes and repeatedly smacked one side of his neck.

He looked at Tess and explained, "If I keep swatting that area the bug won't go there."

"Can you give me some help in here?" Kristen said to Tess in an annoyed voice. Tess guessed she was angry with her for snatching her keycard.

Tess entered the room where she'd delivered Stephen Shelton a couple days ago. He stood facing the window, which only offered a view of the morning darkness. Kristen held one of his hands and was trying to pull him toward the door.

"Help me turn him around," she told Tess.

Tess moved to the front of Stephen and saw he was staring out the window with a dazed expression on his face. She placed a hand on his free arm.

"It's time to go," she said in a soothing voice. She glanced at the entry wound that was visible beneath his remaining hair. She suspected he'd been picking at the scab, which was wet and an angry crimson.

He turned to her. "I'm waiting for the sunrise we watched at the lake house," he said. "Jo was little back then, and Gina was still alive. Alive. Alive. A-"

"Stephen," Kristen snapped.

"Stephen," Tess said, "we're going to take you to a better place."

"You told my daughter and me people get better. Better. So why can't I watch the same sunrise? Jo was little back then, and Gina. Gina."

"We can't bring back the past," Tess said. "But we can work on our future." Her words sounded hollow.

She suddenly wondered how she'd get to Center 7 from Seattle. Taxis didn't venture outside the Secure Territory. And where would she stay once she was in Tacoma?

"Let's go then," Stephen said, allowing the two women to guide him toward the doorway. "Let's find Jo and tell her about the future. Future. Future."

Tess released his hand so Kristen could lead him through the doorway. She spotted the bulge of the redbug beneath the skin of his neck. She'd loathed these insects for taking so many lives, but today she hated them for taking her hope.

As Tess handed out paper cups filled with chewable sedatives to the patients filing into one shuttle, she noticed Yvette carry the antidote container onto the other shuttle. Tess figured Yvette wasn't going to risk there being another attempt to steal the yellow substance.

"Pay attention, Tess," Kristen said. She, too, was distributing tablets to the patients. "You don't want anyone to miss a dose."

Tess wasn't sure why the patients had to be semi-conscious for the ride to the new center. It didn't take long to drive anywhere in the Secure Territory.

When the last patient—a jockish-looking 21-year-old with a blood-encrusted entry wound inside his ear—stepped onto the shuttle, Tess started for the vehicle that held Yvette and Dr. Magnison.

"No," Kristen said, grabbing her arm. "Yvette wants you to ride with me."

Tess nodded and tried to hide her disappointment. She followed Kristen onto the vehicle and sat beside her in the rear. The pale exterminator drove the shuttle, and a bearded exterminator Tess had never seen before sat behind him, watching the rows of drowsy patients.

As the garage door opened to reveal a blindingly sunny day, Tess had the alarming thought that no volunteer or staff member remained in the center to man the watchtower.

Strangely, the leading shuttle didn't head toward the center of the city, where most of the refugee centers were located. It turned onto Westlake Avenue and started down the slope toward Lake Union. Tess's shuttle followed, and soon the vehicles rolled through the No Police Territory.

Tess was surprised that the usually cluttered Westlake Avenue was now clear. No abandoned cars blocked the shuttles' path, and the street even appeared to be free of trash and broken glass. The shuttles passed a parked camouflaged Humvee about every few blocks.

At the bottom of the hill, the shuttles pulled into a parking lot bordering the lake. Tess looked out at the water, which was glittering with the sunlight that was so unusual for November. She saw a dock lined with half-sunken sailboats. She thought she spotted redbugs studding one of the sails like toxic rubies.

A police boat was anchored at the end of the dock. A man in an exterminator suit stepped out of the boat's cabin with a woman who wore no suit or Hazard Wrap.

It was Rachel.

The man waved toward the shuttles and led Rachel along the dock. Rachel watched the wooden planks before her with a forlorn look.

Tess came out of her shock when she felt Kristen poking her arm.

"We have a passenger pick-up," she said. "Come along."

At the front of the shuttle, Kristen reached inside a duffle bag that lay by the driver's seat and removed another paper cup. "I want you to give her the sedatives and take her to a seat," she told Tess. "The exterminators will help you if she tries anything."

Once outside the misting doorway of the shuttle, Tess was relieved that Rachel looked at her with no recognition. She was concealing their newly formed friendship.

"I caught her last night," the man from the police boat told Kristen. "She was trying to hole up inside one of the vessels." He pulled out a folded piece of paper and a pen from his pants pocket. "I just need your authorization."

"The sedatives," Kristen said to Tess before receiving the paper and pen.

"I'd like you to chew these," Tess told Rachel, holding the cup out to her.

Rachel picked up the tablets, and Tess checked to make sure Kristen and the man weren't watching. She looked Rachel in the eyes and subtly shook her head, signaling that she shouldn't consume the tablets.

Rachel nodded. She put the sedatives in her mouth and made a chewing motion.

"I'll show you to your seat," Tess said, slipping her arm around Rachel's. She escorted her onto the shuttle and past the pale and smirking exterminator.

Before Rachel sat, Tess whispered, "They're taking you to a new center. Wherever it is, I'll make sure you don't stay there."

The shuttles continued along a weirdly clear route through the No Police Territory and into Seattle's Eastlake neighborhood. They passed restaurants with smashed windows and overturned tables and chairs inside. A man's corpse dangled by rope from an apartment complex balcony. A couple crows flew out the doorway of a yoga studio.

The shuttles then drove north on the I-5 freeway, which was also unobstructed. Tess guessed the government or some other organization had moved all the wrecked and abandoned vehicles to the weed-infested sides of the road.

Tess saw two large plumes of smoke rising from Northgate Mall's rooftop. She had last visited the mall in early June, when she and her mother bought swimsuits for a fall trip to Palm Springs they never took.

The shuttles exited the freeway and drove along a curving road bordered by forest.

Tess glanced at Rachel. She sat across the aisle, and she was closer to the front of the shuttle. Beside her was an elderly man who'd become blind since a redbug had burrowed beneath his cheek. Tess was relieved Rachel stared directly in front of her, feigning to be as dazed as the rest of the patients.

"You know, we could be in a much worse state."

Tess looked at Kristen. The nurse stared out the window at the road's sun-dappled asphalt.

"That's what I remind myself when things seem really bad," Kristen continued. "Sure, Seattle has suffered a lot. But the government has destroyed cities. I've heard they're doing some kind of firebombing. Yvette told me they bombed Missoula yesterday."

Tess's eyes went round. "But what about the people who are still in those cities?" she asked.

"They get the evacuation warning."

"But there are people," Tess said, nodding toward the shuttle's other passengers, "who wouldn't understand that warning."

Kristen looked at her. "Are they really still human? Or are they more insect?"

"How can you say that?" Tess's voice was loud enough to cause a few patients to lift their lolling heads. The bearded exterminator watched her from the front of the bus with suspicious eyes.

"They're human," Tess said in a softer voice.

The shuttles turned onto a gravel road and drove down a gently sloping hill. The evergreens thinned, and the trees' shadows disappeared from the road as the vehicles entered a valley with dark green pastures separated by orchards that looked like they'd produce much fruit come summer. As the vehicles parked on the side of the road, Tess spotted a distant blue farmhouse and a few grazing white goats. She thought how the patients were fortunate to be entering a refugee center with such an idyllic setting. She wouldn't mind her mother being here.

She saw Dr. Magnison and Yvette leave the other shuttle. Following them were the patients and one of the exterminators, who carried a folding chair and a folding table. They didn't head toward the farmhouse. Instead, they approached a small hill covered in brown, thorny bushes.

The red-faced exterminator was the last to get out of the vehicle, and he neared Tess's shuttle while Dr. Magnison brought his party along a dirt path leading up the hill.

The shuttle's doors opened, and the red-faced exterminator climbed the stairs. "Dr. Magnison's ready for you," he told Kristen. "The other nurse stays here."

Tess felt a burst of pride from the exterminator mistaking her for a nurse. She told herself she practically was one considering all the assistance she'd provided at Center 6. She stood and stepped into the aisle so Kristen could leave the shuttle.

"Why don't you sit in the front and keep an eye on the patients," Kristen said. "We'll come get them soon."

Tess nodded and walked behind Kristen. She avoided looking at Rachel as she passed her. The bearded exterminator rose and motioned for Tess to take his seat. He left the vehicle with the two other exterminators. Tess stood by her new seat while Kristen moved toward the doorway.

"You can call for us if there's a problem," Kristen said, "but don't go far from the shuttle."

Tess nodded and watched her pick up the duffle bag from beside the driver's seat. The bag was unzipped, and Tess thought she spotted a handgun inside. Kristen stepped off the shuttle and walked with the exterminators up the hill.

Tess noticed the bearded exterminator stayed at the top of the hill as if he were serving as guard.

She turned toward the patients and saw that most of them still appeared semi-conscious. A few were dozing. Rachel stared at her with a shocked expression. She began blinking repeatedly.

"Why is everyone drugged?" she asked.

"To keep them calm for the ride to the refugee center." Tess realized her response sounded odd. Where was the refugee center? She didn't see any structure besides the farmhouse. And why was there a gun in the duffle bag? No staff member had ever carried a gun at Center 6.

Tess looked at Stephen Shelton, who sat near her. He was drooling.

"Stephen," she said in a raised voice.

His drooping eyelids slightly lifted.

"Stephen, can you tell me the address of the house where you and your daughter used to live?"

He didn't respond.

"Can you tell me your daughter's name?"

Stephen stayed mute, and Tess wondered why these already impaired patients needed to be even more helpless for the move to their new home.

She glanced up at the hill again. The bearded exterminator remained at his station at the top. He was looking at whatever there was to see on the other side.

"I'm going to find out what's going on," Tess told Rachel. "Can you offer a distraction?"

"What would you like me to do?"

Minutes later, Tess pressed the button for the shuttle doors to open, and Rachel ran out of the vehicle into the sunlight.

"Stop!" Tess shouted in a dramatic voice. She was pleased to see the bearded exterminator turn toward them.

Outside the shuttle, Rachel paused and looked up in the direction of the exterminator. She held a hand behind her back and crossed her fingers as a signal for Tess. She then dashed between the shuttles and headed toward one of the orchards. Tess had told her not to go further than the farmhouse. She didn't want the exterminator to give up on the pursuit and discover that Tess was missing.

As the exterminator approached the shuttle, Tess descended the stairs. "Kristen told me not to leave the patients," she said.

The frowning man didn't even look at her. He ran in the same direction as Rachel, his bulky uniform slowing his movement.

Once he was in the midst of the orchard's trees, Tess hurried toward the hill. She climbed the narrow, winding trail, which was bordered by dry bushes that were about the height of her shoulders.

Near the top, she heard voices coming from close by. She didn't want anyone spotting her. She left the path and crept between bushes, watching out for thorns that might tear her Hazard Wrap. She froze when she saw two figures just feet away from her. She stood on her toes to see better.

Dr. Magnison sat on a large stone at the top of the hill, watching whatever occurred below him. Yvette stood beside him, wringing her gloved hands.

Tess navigated the bushes to get closer to them and see what they saw. The bushes became thin enough to afford a view. She watched Dr. Magnison reach up from his perch on the stone and pat the small of Yvette's back.

"It'll be over soon," he said.

And that's when Tess noticed the line of patients on the path. The pretty forty-something woman from Issaquah stood at the front. Further along the path, Kristen sat at the folding table, which held syringes and a bottle of some substance. The red-faced exterminator stood just behind her with the gun in one hand and an extermination hose coiled at his feet.

"Come along," Kristen called to the woman from Issaquah.

Tess watched Kristen give the woman a shot in her arm and then point along the path to where it ended at a rocky ledge. The other exterminators waited at the end of that path.

The woman from Issaquah shuffled toward the exterminators. She hesitated and glanced back at Kristen. Kristen motioned for her to continue toward the men. The nest person nodded and smiled faintly.

When she reached the exterminators, each man took an arm and swung her over the ledge.

Tess gasped.

She tried to control her panic. She couldn't allow herself to believe what she'd seen. Maybe the exterminators had dropped the woman into water, or some kind of holding area at the entrance of the refugee center.

Tess crouched and continued moving through the bushes, veering around Dr. Magnison and Yvette's position. The downward slope steepened. Tess felt thorns snag her clothing, but all she cared about was what lay past that ledge.

The bushes suddenly ended, and Tess peered into the opening.

Below was a pit filled with what must have been hundreds of bodies. Some of the corpses looked like pale, sleeping people, but most were decaying. Bones protruded, and limbs were bent in unnatural ways. Salt and insecticide foam covered many of the bodies. All wore hospital gowns. Tess recognized the red gowns of Floor 6, the pink gowns of Floor 5, and the blue gowns of Floor 4.

Her mother's floor.

Tess thought she was going to vomit. She turned away from the horrible sight and hurried back through the bushes toward the shuttle. She heard her Hazard Wrap rip, but she didn't check for a tear. As she passed Dr. Magnison and Yvette, she lost control and started sobbing.

She glanced over the bushes and saw Yvette staring at her. The woman's expression showed fear, and then Tess recognized remorse. Tess glared at Yvette with tearing eyes before running through the bushes.

She needed to reach Rachel.

Tess was still crying when she staggered toward the shuttle. She wiped her eyes and glanced around in search of Rachel. She didn't see anyone. The nearest orchard was empty, and goats were the only occupants of the adjacent pasture.

Tess ran back through the open doors of the shuttle, hoping Rachel had returned and was waiting among the patients. But there was no sign of her. The patients remained in their seats and stared at her with glazed eyes that could have belonged to cattle.

"You all need to get off this shuttle now," Tess told them.

The patients continued watching her without emotion.

"Go and hide," Tess shouted. "They're going to kill all of you."

Still failing to trigger a reaction, she went to Stephen Shelton and pulled him up from his seat.

"Your daughter needs you," she said, her voice quivering. She thought of her mother lying in that pit somewhere, perhaps beneath other corpses, and she released another sob. She regained control and guided Stephen down the stairs. He shambled between the vehicles in the direction of the orchard.

Tess had just escorted two other patients out of the shuttle when she heard the exterminator.

"What do you think you're doing?"

It was the red-faced fellow. He strode from the hill, and he carried the gun with him. He formed a fist with his free hand as he neared Tess. "Yvette wants to talk to you," he said.

"Yvette can go to hell!" Tess shrieked.

"Where's Sims?"

Tess guessed he was referring to the bearded exterminator who'd pursued Rachel. "I don't know what happened to him," she said in a faint voice.

The red-faced exterminator moved closer, and she backed up against the side of the shuttle. She winced when she felt the metal. Watching the scowling exterminator, she wondered if she, too, would end up in the pit.

"You sure you don't got a bug in you?" the exterminator asked. "You don't seem to be able to cooperate with people."

"I really don't know where he is," Tess said.

The exterminator reached out and grabbed her throat. The material of her Hazard Wrap didn't offer much protection. She struggled to breathe.

"I should check your neck for a bug bump," the exterminator said, sneering.

"Please." Tess was barely capable of speaking the word. She started to feel dizzy, and she knew she'd faint if she didn't free herself from the man's grip.

She kneed him in the groin, causing his hold to weaken, and she jerked away to the side.

Something ripped. Tess frowned as she glanced down at her shoulder.

The man had torn her Hazard Wrap open, exposing her neck and one shoulder. She could feel the November sunlight on her pale skin.

"You did it to yourself," the exterminator said. "And I've got a feeling that's not the worst of what's going to happen to you."

Tess looked toward the man, and her eyes widened when she saw Rachel standing behind him with a large shovel raised in the air.

The tool came down against the back of the man's helmet, making a cracking sound. The exterminator collapsed on the gravel road. He began to raise himself from the ground, and Rachel hit him again, this time harder. Following a few spasms, his body became still.

"Thank you," Tess rasped, rubbing her throat.

Rachel nodded and gently poked the man's hip with the shovel. He remained motionless. Tess glanced toward the shuttle and saw that some of the patients had actually lifted themselves from their seats to watch the confrontation.

"Where's the other exterminator?" Tess asked Rachel.

"In the barn where I found the shovel. He's in the same way. Way. Way."

Tess squeezed Rachel's shoulder to calm her. "We need to leave this place," she said. She decided not to increase Rachel's stress by telling her about the pit. "But I need to cover up somehow."

The idea came to her instantly.

The antidote.

She would use only a little, and she could take the rest to someone who would ensure it was of immediate benefit to others. Maybe if she made it back to Seattle she could locate Ahmed, and he would suggest someone. He'd said he trusted a certain nurse at Center 3.

Tess motioned for Rachel to accompany her to the second shuttle. As she passed the first, she was grateful to see a few patients standing at the top of the stairs, preparing to venture outside. She wanted to help them, but she knew taking time to do so would probably get her killed.

She glanced toward the hill before opening the shuttle's doors. Thankfully, no one had appeared to look for the missing exterminator.

"I know it's in here somewhere," Tess said as she rushed down the aisle. All the seats were empty, as were the spaces beneath them. "I saw her bring it on board with her."

She glanced up at the overhead compartments. She tried pulling the handle of one, but the compartment was locked. "We need that shovel," she told Rachel.

After prying open the second compartment with the shovel, Tess found the antidote. She set it on a seat and tore off her already ripped sleeve so her left arm was completely bare. She unscrewed the lid of the container and poured a large glob of the yellow substance into her gloved hand. The goo gave off a potent odor that was both sweet and rancid. Tess held her nose as she slathered the antidote over her skin. Rachel helped her apply it to the exposed part of her neck and shoulder.

"Is that enough?" Rachel asked.

Tess shrugged and tried to swallow the knot of fear in her throat. "I don't think anyone can answer that question."

The women were hurrying past the farmhouse when Tess glanced back and spotted someone at the top of the hill. The figure was a thin silhouette pacing back and forth. Tess knew it was Yvette, and she hoped never to see her again.

"Do you hear that?" Rachel whispered. She touched her stomach as if the palm of her hand could somehow protect her unborn baby.

"I've only heard birds," Tess said.

The women had been walking through the woods for almost an hour. Sometimes trails or narrow roads interrupted the forest, but Tess and Rachel never took them. They wanted to avoid all people for now. Tess's arms had begun to ache from lugging the antidote container, and her exposed skin stung from either the foreign substance coating it or the nipping autumn air.

"There it is again. Again."

Tess paused in a cluster of pine trees and listened.

The sound of a car.

"One of the shuttles," Tess said with a frown. She recognized the sound of the engine. She looked at Rachel as the noise increased. "It's coming toward us."

"But how could they find us?" Rachel asked.

And then Tess knew.

A tracker chip. Exterminators used them in the field to locate one another, and refugee center workers attached them to center equipment to prevent theft. Yvette was particularly paranoid about the loss of the ECG machines and x-ray equipment she and Dr. Magnison had purchased with their own money.

Tess lifted the antidote container. On its underside was a chip the size of a quarter.

She heard doors slamming and men's voices. She had little time.

She found a stick and used it to scrape off the chip. She picked up the piece of metal from the forest floor and handed Rachel the antidote container. She pointed in the direction from which they'd come.

"Go back to those ferns we walked through and lie down in the center of them," she said. "I'll come find you."

Rachel gave her a doubting look.

"Go now!" Tess said. After Rachel took off through the woods, Tess headed the opposite way. She would get rid of the tracker chip and circle back to find Rachel.

She heard the snapping of tree branches behind her. She glanced toward the noise and thought she spotted an exterminator's helmet between two distant trees.

Tess tossed the tracker chip in the men's direction, and then she hurried toward the thick trunk of a cedar tree. She sat beneath that tree and made herself as small as possible by wrapping her arms around her shins and resting her chin on her knees. She knew the men would never see her so long as they didn't move beyond the chip.

"They've gotta be around here," one of the men said. Tess recognized the pale exterminator's voice. "The signal's a lot stronger."

"It's coming from over here," a woman said. It was Kristen who spoke.

Tess heard boots crunching in her direction. She held her breath.

"Look!" another man said. "They ditched the chip. Let's tell the others. We can all fan out through the forest."

They didn't come closer.

Tess listened to their voices fade among the trees. She closed her eyes and sighed.

A tickling sensation made her open them again.

She saw a redbug resting on the yellow crust covering her forearm. The insect was the length of a finger and purplish red. Its feelers touched her skin as if they were inspecting it.

Tess felt the scream filling her chest. She attempted to remain silent and motionless so she wouldn't attract those who searched for her.

She knew if the antidote didn't work she'd have about 24 hours to live. She wondered how the toxin would take her. Would she have a fever first? Or a rash inching along her arm? Maybe she'd succumb to seizures before having either of those symptoms.

She suddenly remembered what her mother had told her at her father's memorial. Tess had been struggling to stop crying and keep breathing, and her mother gripped her hand tightly.

"Believe it or not, this is a new beginning."

Tess watched the redbug flap its wings. The insect lifted and vanished in the dimming late-afternoon sky. Tess was terrified of dying, but then she considered what she'd do if she stayed alive.

BOOK3
POPULATION CONTROL

An excerpt of minutes from the First Convention on Red-bug-Borne Illness (RBI):

The Boise Delegate agreed that research on RBI is essential, but he suggested the Department of Health and Human Services officially categorize so-called "nest people" as a vulnerable population. He stated that this low status group is subject to exploitation by researchers. The San Francisco Delegate argued that such official categorization is unnecessary, as anyone currently living in the northwestern United States is part of a vulnerable population.

I. CLIFFORD STOWE, CHA

"You guys have to go again?" Cliff asked as the two exterminators donned their helmets. He sat in the Humvee's first row of seats. Beside him was Waverley, an 18-year-old nest person they should never have picked up on the outskirts of Tacoma.

"You're the one who gave us the coffee," Ted told Cliff. He'd been driving the vehicle since they left Harborview Medical Center, where Cliff had worked as a study coordinator in the Redbug Research Unit for the past six months.

Rand, the other exterminator, pointed through the windshield at the street, which was lined with leafy, thick-trunked trees and the occasional ornate gate that led to a sprawling property. Spring had caused daffodils and tulips of various colors to raise their bright heads along the sidewalks.

"I can't think of a nicer place to piss," Rand said. "Tony neighborhood, eh?"

Cliff sank back into his seat with a sigh, and Ted pulled his key out of the ignition. He dangled the ring of keys over the middle of the front seat and joked, "I'm taking these so you guys don't make a getaway."

Cliff shook his head in annoyance. The two exterminators left the Humvee.

Cliff knew he should just be grateful they were driving him to Portland, where he was going to start a position as a coordinator for a massive blood sampling study involving nest people and those who'd died as a result of redbug toxin. But he wanted the exterminators to move more quickly. They'd spent 45 minutes on the side of the freeway with Waverley, trying to figure out whether she had any living family or friends and if she wanted them to deliver her to a refugee center in Portland.

The main reason to hurry was the possibility of bombings in western Washington. Just before Harborview had shut down, Cliff and his co-workers heard rumors about the government bombing Spokane and smaller cities east of the Cascades. The government announced two weeks ago that due to the unrelenting redbug infestation, it was dissolving Seattle's Secure Territory and urging occupants to immediately leave the state. Homeland Security would be closing all refugee centers and moving all exterminator teams to Oregon and California. Most of the Secure Territory's occupants were gone by the time Cliff and the exterminators drove south.

Cliff doubted the government would destroy the cities of western Washington, which had been so densely populated before the redbug invasion, but he was still nervous about the idea.

He watched Ted and Rand standing side by side half a block away from the Humvee, urinating into a hedge speckled with pink flowers. The men's sloping shoulders showed how relaxed they were. Cliff wouldn't have been surprised if one of them was whistling.

"Dad, are we going to check into the hotel before we go see the fountain, fountain?"

Cliff shot a surprised look at Waverley. She was staring at him with those large, green eyes that showed too much trust. She had pale blonde hair that almost reached her waist. She wore a yellow sweater ripped in various places and jeans stained by dirt. Her redbug entry wound was in the form of a wide but subtle scab beneath her chin. The bulge of the insect was in the center of her neck, like some malformed Adam's apple.

"I'd like to put on my new sandals if we're going to be walking all over Rome," she said.

"I'm not your dad," Cliff said, patting her shoulder. He turned away from her, not wanting to seem overly empathetic. As a study coordinator, he'd learned the risks of emotional attachment with nest people. He looked back out the window at the urinating exterminators and added, "And we're not in Rome."

Cliff had interacted with hundreds of nest people while coordinating studies at Harborview, but few of them had exhibited this sort of disorientation, which seemed to make Waverley think she was in the distant past. He suspected his appearance had made her associate him with her father. Cliff was only 40, but his hair had changed from salt-and-pepper to a uniform gray over the past year. Also contributing to his aged look was his pasty skin, which hadn't received much natural light in six months.

He remembered how Viola had told him on their first date that she thought of him as "The Pale Fox." She said she'd wanted him to ask her out as soon as she saw him come into the government-subsidized cafe where she worked as a barista.

But no, Cliff wasn't going to think about Viola. He needed to remain in his unemotional bubble and get to Portland.

"We could sit on the Spanish Steps and have a snack," Waverley said. "Isn't our hotel right near there? There? There? There?"

Cliff looked at Waverley again and saw she was staring in the direction of the exterminators. He glanced outside the window and spotted a masculine-looking figure sneaking up behind the men. The person was covered in what appeared to be a patchwork of dark green garbage bags held together with duct tape. He wore goggles and a red Mexican wrestler's mask. A long, black ponytail protruded from beneath the rear of the mask like some animal's tail.

The man raised a shotgun and fired into the middle of Ted's back, sending the exterminator crashing into the flowery hedge.

"No," Cliff gasped.

He watched Rand reel around. The gunman aimed at his face shield.

Cliff shut his eyes as the explosion sounded. He heard Waverley whimpering. "We need to get out of here," he told her. He reached past her with a shaking hand and opened the door leading to the street. "Go. Now!"

Before leaving the vehicle, he pulled up the portion of his Hazard Wrap that would cover his head.

Cliff and Waverley had just reached the sidewalk across the street when the gunman hollered, "I'm coming for you next!"

Waverley paused, and Cliff yanked her toward the nearby street corner. As they rounded the ivy wall bordering that corner, Cliff glanced back and saw the gunman was running in their direction. Cliff felt his heart hammering inside his ribcage.

He looked at the flat stretch of sidewalk ahead of them. He was relieved to see a driveway with a partially open gate. He led Waverley past that gate and shut it behind them as quietly as possible. Their pursuer still hadn't come around the corner.

The driveway led a distance to a Spanish-style mansion that didn't belong under the metal-gray skies of the Northwest. The house was a muted pink and had red-tile roofing and numerous balconies. Bloom-less rose bushes lined the driveway, and to the left of those bushes was an expansive lawn that looked as if it hadn't been mowed in months. On the far side of the grass was a large gazebo with a tiled roof. Trees lined the front and sides of the property. Cliff thought he spotted the blue-black waters of the Puget Sound behind the house.

He didn't look for long because he and Waverley needed to hide. He led her into the trees until the foliage was thick enough to conceal them from anyone on the sidewalk.

While they crouched in the greenery, Cliff felt Waverley place a hand on his back. She nodded in the direction of the house and whispered, "Is that the hotel?"

"No," he responded more loudly than he should have. His voice revealed his irritation. He sidestepped out of her touch. He thought how he shouldn't be here with her. He should be up in Canada, with Viola.

They'd planned the weeklong vacation on their fourth date, which occurred in late February. They would go in April, when everything was in bloom. Cliff said they could hitch rides to and from Vancouver with exterminators. He knew many of the teams because they transported nest people from the refugee centers to the Redbug Research Unit. Before leaving the taxi they shared, Viola kissed him with those full, red lips and whispered, "Maybe we'll just never come back."

But she never returned after that fourth date. Or at least the Viola Cliff had known and fallen in love with never did.

"Dad?"

Cliff snapped out of his remembrance and felt Waverley tugging the sleeve of his Hazard Wrap.

"I think he's here for our suitcases, suitcases," she said.

Cliff peered through the trees and saw the boots of a man approaching them across the grass. Cliff rose out of his crouching position, preparing to flee with Waverley through the trees.

But he remained still when he saw that the figure who pushed his way through the foliage wasn't the gunman. This fellow was short and stocky, and he wore an exterminator uniform. One side of his helmet was covered in burn marks.

As the man neared, Cliff noticed the brown moustache through the face shield and the yellowish eyes that seemed to examine Waverley from head to foot. The man appeared to be in his mid-thirties.

He looked at Cliff and asked, "Do you folks need help?"

Cliff and Waverley followed the short man through the mansion's front doorway into a high-ceilinged foyer. The floor was composed of maroon and white tiles, and an enormous marble statue of a winged horse stood on its hind legs in the middle of the hall. Cliff was surprised by the words painted in red on one side of the horse:

RIDE TO THE SKY

But he was more concerned about his and Waverley's safety. He glanced out one of the foyer's window panels to make sure their pursuer wasn't ascending the house's front stairs.

"Someone shot the men who drove us down here from Seattle," he told the short man. "They're dead. They were exterminators."

The man paused and turned back toward them. He gave Waverley another one of those looks, as if he were measuring more than just her beauty.

Cliff wanted to end the man's awkward silence. "My name's Cliff, and this is Waverley. What's your name?"

The man's eyes briefly met Cliff's. "Rufus."

"Did you serve as an exterminator? You've got the uniform."

Rufus shook his head and led them past the horse statue.

"Is this your house?" Cliff asked, trying not to reveal his doubt. He imagined someone older and stately owning a place as enormous as this.

"It belongs to Nathaniel Eagleston," Rufus said in a stern voice. "I'm taking you to him."

They walked from the foyer into a living room filled with more expensive-looking possessions in odd locations: two tan sofas in a V-position in front of a fireplace, crystal lamps encircling a mattress, oil portraits of middle-aged and elderly people hanging upside down. Windows lined one side of the room, offering an idyllic view of a turquoise pool and blooming gardens and, in the distance, the now sunlit Puget Sound. No sealant covered those windows to protect against redbugs.

Cliff spotted someone's head break through the surface of the pool.

Rufus pushed open one of the living room's French doors and motioned for Cliff and Waverley to enter the backyard.

Waverley hesitated near the door and turned to Cliff. "Do you really want to wander through the city without a map? Especially with all these beggars and thieves around?"

Cliff gave Rufus an apologetic look. He tapped a finger against his head. "Forgive her," he said. "She's-"

"I know what she is," Rufus said, watching Waverley again.

Cliff hooked his arm around Waverley's and led her outside. To the right of them was a small pool house, also in the Spanish style, flanked by a pair of sickly looking palm trees. Cliff's eyes lingered on black spots speckling one of the tree trunks. The spots resembled redbug feces.

"Those trees will get healthier."

The voice came from the pool. Cliff glanced at the speaker, who was treading water.

"Are you Nathaniel?" he asked, his surprise apparent in his voice. The darkly tanned figure in the pool couldn't have been older than 21. His wet hair was sandy and shoulder-length. He had light blue eyes and high cheekbones that gave him a WASP-y handsomeness, but there was something unsettling, something unsound, in his gaze.

"The climate's going to change even faster when we're fully in the new order of things," he said, nodding toward the palm trees, "and Washington will get hotter than California. The bugs are just one sign of the changes ahead."

Cliff forced a polite grin. "Maybe so." Wanting to avoid the weird topic of conversation, he asked, "You own this house?"

"Of course I do." Nathaniel sounded annoyed. "My dad's not around anymore, and the son inherits from the father." He placed his lean yet muscular arms on the edge of the pool and lifted his dripping body out of the water.

He was naked and bronzed all over.

Cliff wondered why Nathaniel would make himself so vulnerable to insects, unless he was as mentally off as he sounded.

"So you're someone important," Nathaniel said as Rufus fetched him a towel that lay on a tipped-over stone bench. "Ruf only brings me important people."

"I wouldn't say I'm important," Cliff said, looking away from Nathaniel's naked body. "My name's Cliff. I help doctors do research on redbug toxin and nest people. I was working at Harborview Medical Center, up in Seattle, before the government told everyone to leave the city. I met Waverley here on the way to Portland."

He glanced at Waverley, who stood beside him. She appeared to be in a daze, and her lips trembled slightly.

"That can be a gift, you know," Nathaniel said.

"I'm sorry?" Cliff asked. He looked back at Nathaniel, who now wrapped the towel around his waist.

"Being a nest person," Nathaniel said, the irritation returning to his voice. "I mean it can turn you into someone greater."

Cliff looked at Rufus to see if he, too, recognized the craziness in Nathaniel's words. Rufus's eyes only showed respect for the young man.

"Listen," Cliff told Nathaniel. "We just want to be safely on our way. Someone shot the two exterminators who were driving us to Portland. I need to get down there to help with another study. Do you know how we can access a vehicle?"

"So you know all about nest people, don't you?" Nathaniel asked.

Cliff tried not to reveal his impatience. "I know a lot about them." He remembered the day Viola had come back into his life. She filed into the Redbug Research Unit's hospital wing with a group of nest people bused in from Center 4. Cliff attempted to force back his tears when he spotted the entry wound on her elegantly curving neck.

Nathaniel suddenly gripped Cliff's shoulder. "If you know about nest people then you are important to me. I'll need you here for just one night. You can leave tomorrow. I can give you the keys to one of the neighbor's cars." Smirking, he added, "Now that everyone's gone I've got access to everything."

Cliff didn't want to spend the night. Nathaniel was too weird for his liking, and staying in the area would be dangerous. "Did you know the government's been bombing cities and towns in eastern Washington?" he asked. "I wouldn't be surprised if they started bombing west of the mountains any time now."

Nathaniel gave Rufus a knowing smile. "We've heard. Have you heard the bombs don't do a damn thing? To the bugs, I mean. They're tougher than roaches, roaches."

Cliff's body tensed up when he heard the repetition. Was that what was wrong with Nathaniel? Was that why he didn't care about being naked outside? He was a nest person? Cliff tried to locate the redbug entry wound, but he saw no mark on Nathaniel's face or neck. He guessed the wound was on the back of his neck, beneath his damp hair.

"Everything's evolving," Nathaniel said. "The bugs. The nest people. Of course, a shitload of people are dying. But that's the natural order of things."

Cliff wished he could get inside that car immediately. He looked at Waverley, who appeared to be more frightened than before. He told Nathaniel, "I really think we should go now. Waverley was pretty traumatized by what happened to those exterminators. I'd like to get her to a place where she can feel settled."

"This is that place," Nathaniel said. "She'll feel like she's part of the gang. Won't she, Ruf?"

Rufus nodded. Once again, his eyes were on Waverley.

"Let's introduce them to the girls," Nathaniel said.

After donning a white robe covered in what appeared to be paint splotches, Nathaniel led Cliff and Waverley up a short external staircase on one side of the house. Rufus followed in the rear.

Cliff kept his arm around Waverley's. Her fear seemed to have subsided, and she moved up the stairs as if she were sleep-walking. Cliff once again looked for a redbug entry wound on Nathaniel, but his hair still blocked the nape of his neck.

The stairs brought them to a sunlit deck with a table set for one. Beside the silverware and empty plate was a wine glass filled to the brim. A lengthy mirror lay in the center of the deck.

Cliff let go of Waverley's arm and looked through the stretch of trees that paralleled the side of the house. He was able to discern a blue mansion with a sloping lawn as unkempt as this house's. He thought he spotted a shriveled, darkened corpse on a distant patch of the grass.

"Girls?" Nathaniel called.

Cliff turned from the neighboring property to the doorway that led from the deck to the house. Two attractive, slender women stepped through that doorway. Both wore short-sleeved gray-and-white maids' uniforms that reached to just above their knees. They had on dark red lipstick and heavy black eyeliner that made Cliff think of raccoons' eyes.

"This is Rachel," Nathaniel said, pointing to the red-haired woman on the left. She stared blankly ahead of her with big hazel eyes. Cliff guessed she was a nest person when he spotted the purplish scar below her earlobe.

"And Miyoko," Nathaniel said. Miyoko actually looked at Cliff and smiled. She had short, dark hair that framed her lovely oval face. Just beside a beauty mark on her left cheek was a pink Band-Aid that covered most of a redbug entry wound. Cliff saw that the index finger of her right hand was twitching.

Miyoko came to Nathaniel and handed him a pair of pricey-looking sunglasses. She asked, "Would you like your lunch now, sir?"

"Not yet." Nathaniel retrieved the glass of wine from the table and sipped the red liquid before sitting in the center of the mirror. "There are three other girls," he told Cliff. "Heather, Daphne, and Sheryl. Sheryl's sick at the moment. You know how that can happen with nest people. And of course we've lost girls when the bugs came out of them."

Cliff frowned and asked, "So you're keeping these women here?"

"'Keeping'?" Nathaniel said. "They help me, and I help them. Right, Ruf?"

Rufus nodded. "You feed them. You give them shelter in a house that has electricity."

"We've got a generator," Nathaniel said, his pride apparent in his voice. "The girls have their own bedrooms, and they're welcome to stay in the pool house when they want—like when they're sick. They have that place all to themselves. We never go in there."

"Never," Rufus said.

Nathaniel lay back on the mirror and put on the sunglasses. He stared up at the blue sky. "I have to treat the girls well," he said. "They're my first followers. In the new order of things, I'm going to have lots and lots more. Millions. Billions. But you've got to start with a base."

Cliff felt a cold sweat coming through his pores, making him uncomfortable in his Hazard Wrap. He needed to escape this craziness. "Waverley," he said, "we're leaving now."

"Nope," Nathaniel said in a forceful voice.

Cliff winced at the denial. He saw that Rufus blocked the stairs.

"Miyoko," Nathaniel said, "bring Waverley up to her room. She'll sleep where Veronique used to."

Cliff watched Miyoko take Waverley's hand and steer her toward the doorway. Waverley looked back at him and asked, "Will we meet at the Coliseum?"

Cliff tried to think of how they could escape. He considered jumping off the deck to the driveway below and running away on his own, but he'd already formed that emotional attachment to Waverley he'd originally wanted to avoid.

He turned to Nathaniel. "And now you're going to keep us here, too?"

"I'm going to keep you overnight so you can do a favor for me, and then tomorrow you're free. But first, you'll have a rest. Ruf, put him in the room where I had my stepmom stay."

"Are you sure you want him in there?" Rufus asked.

"Don't I know where everyone belongs in the order of things?"

Rufus nodded obediently.

As Rufus led him into the house, Cliff noticed Rachel look directly at him. Her eyes were no longer blank.

"Is Waverley on the same floor as me?" Cliff asked Rufus as they climbed a spiraling staircase within the house.

Rufus didn't respond. He brought Cliff into a hallway featuring a sloppily painted mural. The left side of the mural showed a man and a redbug of equal proportions. Above them were a yellow sun and its protruding rays. To the right of that depiction, the man and the redbug were inside the sun. And at the end of the mural, the man and the redbug had disappeared and the sun had become enormous and blood red. Its rays reached the ceiling and floor.

Below the final sun someone had written *AND SO IT SHALL BE.*

"People will be coming for me," Cliff said. "Those exterminators who drove us down here had tracker chips in their uniforms. Homeland Security will know something went wrong." He doubted the government would actually send help, but he hoped he'd sounded convincing nonetheless.

Rufus acted as if he hadn't heard a word. He opened a door to their left and motioned for Cliff to enter. "Nathaniel's letting you spend the night here and telling you how to get a car tomorrow," he said. "I think you can do him one favor in return."

Cliff hesitated before walking inside the bedroom. He frowned. "Was this Nathaniel's stepmother's room? Where is she now?"

Rufus turned away and shut the door, leaving him inside the bedroom.

Cliff heard the sound of the door's lock.

The bedroom was in a corner of the house and offered windows on two walls. A queen-sized bed with a pink comforter was against a windowless wall. Also in the room were a dresser and a white wooden chair. Cliff found a small bathroom attached to the bedroom. The bathroom contained a shower, a sink, and a toilet, which Cliff used after lifting his Hazard Wrap above his waist.

While urinating, he gazed with tired eyes at the shower curtain's little orange and yellow flowers. He thought how he'd never be here if Ted and Rand hadn't pulled over on the nearby street to relieve themselves. He realized he'd known so little about the men. Were they married? Did they have families? Who would want to know about their deaths?

Cliff had avoided getting close with people after Viola's time in the study. Intimacy was just too risky. He remembered having nightmares while she'd been hospitalized at the Redbug Research Unit. He repeatedly dreamt about coming into work and opening the door of her room to find that a long, writhing cluster of redbugs had replaced her sleeping body.

Dr. Johns, the investigator, had insisted she stay in the trial. "I know it's awkward for you to take her vital signs every morning," he told Cliff. "But she's greatly contributing to society's knowledge about what those insects can do to people."

Cliff recalled that, in addition to having horrible dreams, he'd begun weeping in his apartment after work each day. And then there was the time his hand had started shaking while he was drawing Viola's blood. The needle broke. She only stared back at him with those empty eyes and asked, "Ouch?"

Cliff scrubbed his hands in the bathroom sink and rinsed his face with hot water. The mirror above the sink showed his eyes were bloodshot and his skin was an even sicklier white than usual.

He moved to one window and looked down at the backyard. Beyond the garden was a copse of evergreens and a rocky beach sloping to the Puget Sound. There was also a pier with a small rowboat tied to its end.

He noticed movement by the pool house. He spotted Rachel, the redheaded nest person he'd met on the deck. She was carrying a large woven basket filled with what appeared to be cans of food. She glanced at the house, as if she were making sure no one was watching her.

Cliff thought maybe "the girls" were somewhat respected on this property. He'd originally suspected that Nathaniel and Rufus were exploiting them, but if the girls moved about the house and yard on their own then perhaps they had some autonomy. As much autonomy as a nest person could have.

The nest people in the studies hadn't been the freest of beings. They weren't allowed to leave the hospital once the study had begun, and about 20% of them would die in their small rooms during the course of the trial. Once they'd completed their participation, they returned to their original refugee centers—other institutional settings with sleep-deprived staff members and lousy food.

Cliff was going to have Viola move into his apartment after she completed the study. He'd told her this the last time he took her pulse, but her heart rate remained the same throughout her hearing the news. She responded by saying, "I told my new boyfriend I could take a trip to Canada, Canada in April, but I have my doubts, doubts."

As Cliff watched Rachel disappear inside the pool house, he rested his forehead against the windowpane. He clamped his eyes shut and forced the sadness back down into the pit of his gut. He told himself to stop thinking about Viola. That had been the plan for when he left Seattle.

Quit dwelling on what happened.

Stay inside an unemotional bubble.

Go to Portland and conduct a study that will involve the processing of blood samples and no direct interaction with patients.

Survive this.

Cliff heard something knock against the windowpane.

It was a redbug three times the size of any he'd seen before.

He stepped backwards until he tripped over the chair. He regained his balance and watched the insect with revulsion.

The redbug was about 10 inches long and a few inches wide. He could see the brown ovals of its eyes and even the black hairs on its legs. At the end of its body was a thorn-like stinger—something redbugs weren't supposed to have. Its antennae touched the windowpane searchingly for some seconds, and then it flew back toward the garden.

Cliff cautiously tiptoed to the window and looked down into the yard again. He observed about a dozen of the gigantic redbugs resting on one wall of the pool house. None of the insects moved. They appeared to be waiting and watching for something.

He remembered Nathaniel's words: "Everything's evolving. The bugs. The nest people."

He lowered the blinds of both windows and staggered to the bed, where he collapsed on the pink comforter. He pulled off his Hazard Wrap so he wore only a light green V-neck sweater and khakis. He questioned whether he should try to escape. After all, he was momentarily safe in a comfortable enough bedroom with a view of the Puget Sound. And outside were plus-sized bugs and a killer lurking around in a bodysuit made of garbage bags.

And nowhere would he find Viola.

He thought of that nurse who'd burst into his office and told him about Viola jumping out of one of Harborview's seventh-floor windows.

"I'm so sorry," she'd said after Cliff shot up from his chair. "And Dr. Johns told me she was pregnant."

"She was pregnant?" Cliff felt as if the floor beneath his feet was collapsing.

Just before falling asleep on the bed, he repeated inside his head, *Quit dwelling on what happened. Quit dwelling on what happened. Quit dwelling....*

The sound of an airplane woke Cliff.

He cracked open his eyes and found that twilight's purple darkness had seeped inside the bedroom. He left the bed and slowly raised the blinds of the western window. The sky outside was a dark pink. The plane sounded like it was flying east of the mansion. His body became rigid when he thought of the plane coming to bomb the area.

But no, he'd heard the government arranged for deathly silent drones to drop the bombs. That way no pilot had to cope with the guilt.

He grew excited at the idea that this was a rescue plane. Maybe someone really had noticed that Ted and Rand's tracker chips hadn't moved in the last eight hours. Surely, the rescuers would check out the houses near the abandoned Humvee to look for him. He didn't have a tracker chip in his Hazard Wrap, but a number of people had known about his driving south with the exterminators.

Cliff glanced around the room for a lamp. He wanted to make the bedroom as bright as possible. The more light, the greater the chance rescuers would knock on the mansion's front door.

He saw a lamp on the end of the dresser—just within reach of the bed. He sat near the bed's headboard and fumbled around the lamp's base in search of a switch.

The lamp suddenly cast a rosy glow in the room. Cliff was about to look for a switch on the wall to turn on the ceiling light, but he stopped moving when he saw the little red spots covering the strip of wall between the bed and the dresser.

Dried blood splatter.

The spots near the dresser were larger than the others. He left the bed so he'd have better leverage for moving the dresser. As he pulled the furniture away from the wall, he watched the blood splatter turn into one continuous, dried smear that spanned the length of the dresser.

And nailed over that smear was a pale blue dress. There were bloodstains on the material, centering around a tear in the chest area.

Nauseous, Cliff almost pushed the dresser back into place. But then he spotted the framed photograph leaning against the wall. He picked up the frame and saw its glass covering was cracked. The picture beneath the glass showed an adolescent Nathaniel standing next to a pretty woman in her forties with big blonde hair. Nathaniel wore a brown blazer and a tie, and the woman wore the same blue dress that was nailed to the wall. Though she had her arm around Nathaniel's waist, she smiled coolly at the camera. Someone had penned the word *TRAITOR* along the bottom of the frame.

Cliff recalled he was in the room where Nathaniel's step-mother had stayed. He set the photograph back into its place with an unsteady hand. He was about to start inspecting the drawers of the dresser when the knock sounded at his door.

"Nathaniel's ready for you," Rufus said.

"Just a minute!" Cliff called. He dreaded Rufus learning of his discovery. But what if Nathaniel wanted him to find the blood-encrusted dress? After all, he was the one who'd arranged for Cliff to be in this room. And if that was the case, did Nathaniel want to send him some message about his and Waverley's fates?

Cliff quickly pushed the dresser against the wall and came around the bed to stand in front of the door. He wiped sweat from his forehead while Rufus unlocked the door.

"We're going upstairs," Rufus told him. "You won't need to put on your Hazard Wrap." Rufus had removed his exterminator uniform and replaced it with a gray suit that was too large for him. He'd also gelled back his brown hair, revealing his receding hairline. "Turn off that lamp," he added. "We try to conserve as much electricity as possible so we don't tax the generator."

Cliff nodded and forced a polite smile. As he clicked off the light, he tried not to worry about leaving this room without protective clothing. What was most important was that he and Waverley escape from the mansion tonight.

Cliff was surprised he was meeting with Nathaniel on the top floor of the house rather than downstairs. Rufus brought him along a hallway with flickering candles suspended from its walls. The hardwood floor was littered with glittering objects: piles of coins, assorted silverware, strands of jewelry, a few goblets.

"What is all this?" Cliff asked.

"Offerings," Rufus said. He didn't glance back at Cliff when he spoke. "For Nathaniel's passage."

Cliff frowned at the nonsensical reply. He saw they'd reached a set of doors at the end of the hallway. As Rufus turned the doorknob, Cliff questioned whether he might die inside this room. He was considering running back down the hallway when he saw Miyoko standing in the room with a champagne glass in her hand. She still wore her maid's uniform.

"For you," she said, raising the glass and smiling at him.

Rufus opened both doors and then stood against the door-frame, waiting for him to enter.

Cliff received the glass and ventured inside the space.

He faced a king-sized bed and a night table supporting burning red candles. To the left of the bed was a recliner chair. Someone had parked a dinner tray near the chair and loaded it with a glass of water, a fork, a napkin, and a steaming plate of lasagna. The smell of the food made Cliff's stomach grumble. He recalled he hadn't eaten in almost 10 hours.

Someone moved in the shadows beyond the chair, and Cliff noticed Nathaniel watching him from near a windowed door that led to a balcony. Nathaniel wore a black robe. The dim lighting made him look as if he had empty eye sockets.

"Come here," he told Cliff.

Cliff was nervous about approaching. He knew he should be fleeing through the hallway. He saw Rufus and Miyoko watching him.

"I want to show you something before you eat," Nathaniel said. He pointed toward the balcony. Night was falling outside, but Cliff could still discern the distant shapes of skyscrapers rising beyond the trees of this neighborhood.

"Tacoma," Nathaniel said. "My dad owned about a quarter of the commercial real estate in the city. Now it's just a bunch of dark, burnt-out buildings, buildings. The old order has become powerless."

Cliff took a step away from Nathaniel. He remembered the dress downstairs. "What happened to your dad?"

"Eat your dinner," Nathaniel said, motioning toward the chair. "I'll bet you're starving."

Indeed, Cliff's hunger was even greater than his fear. He decided he could use the food to maintain his strength. He sat in the chair and immediately forked lasagna into his mouth. The hot meal tasted heavenly.

"Thank you," he managed to say between bites.

"Miyoko made it for you," Nathaniel said.

Cliff looked at Miyoko and offered a grateful smile. Her index finger was twitching again. She nodded politely and left the room.

"This is my bedroom," Nathaniel said. "It used to be my dad and my stepmom's."

Cliff paused in his chewing at the mention of the stepmother.

"I'd have you eat in the dining room, but I need you to do that favor for me in here. This is the safest place in the house. You see, there are...beings after me. They're against my passage."

Cliff set the fork on the tray. "I don't understand. Are you going somewhere?"

Nathaniel gave a slanted grin and looked from Cliff to Rufus and back again, as if he were amused by Cliff's ignorance. He pointed at the ceiling and said, "I'm going to ascend."

Cliff stared at him dumbly. He considered getting out of the chair, but he figured Rufus would easily block him if he tried leaving the room.

"You'll understand in a minute," Nathaniel continued. "I'm transforming. I'm going to rise above the rest of the world and at the same time be everywhere."

"Okay." Cliff sounded skeptical.

"Don't worry," Nathaniel said, "I'm used to doubters. My dad questioned me when I left Seattle University and told him I had a calling to be a visual artist. He wanted me to be a lawyer and follow the usual track, track, track."

Cliff noticed Rufus giving Nathaniel a look of concern.

"And my stepmom," Nathaniel said, shaking his head. "You know how she was, Ruf."

Rufus nodded.

Nathaniel removed the dinner tray from in front of Cliff. Cliff suddenly regretted not finishing the food.

"Ruf was my family's pool cleaner," Nathaniel said, carrying the tray toward one corner of the room. "He became my best friend. My stepmom found out he'd been a chemical soldier in the Iran War, and she told my dad she didn't want 'that sort of man' working around our house. She said 'that sort of man' became unstable, unstable. I tried telling her how Rufus was a more than decent human being, but she never listened."

Nathaniel hurled the tray against the wall. The glass exploded, and the plate and fork fell to the floor with a clatter. Gobs of lasagna bled down the wall.

Cliff winced at the sight.

"But Ruf and I showed them, them," Nathaniel said. "I was the son with mental issues and Ruf was the pool cleaner with the past, and now look at us, us. Ruf is guardian of the estate and the girls, and I'm going to ascend, ascend, ascend." Nathaniel's eyes blinked repeatedly.

"Rachel!" Rufus shouted. The call made Nathaniel stop blinking and stare ahead of him.

Cliff watched Rachel hurry in from the hallway. Like Miyoko, she wore her maid's uniform. She wheeled in a tall, white medical lamp, which she positioned in front of Cliff's chair, where the dinner tray had been. She kneeled and plugged the lamp's cord into an outlet, causing the lamp's bulb to emit a bright light.

Cliff thought Rachel was looking into his eyes, but then her gaze went blank, as if she were pretending not to be aware of him.

"Tell me, Cliff," Nathaniel said, coming near them. "Does Rachel seem different from most nest people?" He placed a hand on the woman's shoulder.

Cliff's eyes met Rachel's, and he watched emotion replace the former emptiness. He was certain she was signaling for him to say no.

"She's like most nest people I've seen," he lied for her. He was relieved to have made this slightest of connections with someone in the house.

Nathaniel shrugged. "Maybe it's her red hair that sets her apart from the other girls for me. My real mom had red hair. She died when I was 9. You can go, Rachel."

Cliff looked toward Nathaniel, and the lamplight made him squint. "I'd like to leave this house now. Please. I can get you money if that would help."

Nathaniel laughed. "Like I need more of that," he said. "My dad was practically bursting with it." He stepped closer to Cliff and turned his back to him. He lowered himself until he was on both knees and the light shone on the rear of his head and neck. With one hand, he parted strands of his sandy hair.

Cliff saw a redbug entry wound beneath the hair. The wound was a purplish scar in the shape of a crescent moon.

"How long have you been a nest person?" he asked in a matter-of-fact voice.

Nathaniel turned to him. "But you see I'm not just a nest person."

"I don't see," Cliff said, his annoyance surfacing.

"It was in mid-September when the bug came to me," Nathaniel said. "The insects hadn't yet invaded western Washington, and people were still going outside without Hazard Wraps. I was on the front lawn when I felt the bug crawling up my neck. I'd just been arguing with my dad and stepmom. They'd given Ruf his notice."

Cliff tried to look at Rufus, but the room's dimness concealed the man's expression.

"There was a sharp stinging when it first broke my skin, skin," Nathaniel continued. "I cried out. But as it dug deeper inside me I heard a voice say, 'We've chosen you. You're going to be different from the others. You're going to rise above them all.'"

Cliff had heard countless nest people's delusions, but this was the first delusion of grandeur. "So what do you want from me?" he asked.

Nathaniel stood and pulled down his robe to reveal his lower back. "You're the expert on nest people. Tell me I really did overpower the bug." He reached behind him and touched the base of his spine.

Cliff spotted a bulge just above Nathaniel's right buttock. The bulge was about the length of a redbug.

"Use the light to see better," Nathaniel said.

Cliff adjusted the lamp. He could make out the insect beneath the skin, but it was a grayish brown color. The redbug's legs were curled beneath its body.

"It's dead, isn't it?" Nathaniel asked.

Despite his reluctance, Cliff pressed one finger against the flesh. The insect didn't move. "I believe it is," he said.

"I've overpowered it," Nathaniel said. "Have you ever seen that happen before?"

Cliff hadn't. The redbugs either left the nest person's body at some point or died after the nest person was deceased. "This is an anomaly," he said.

"I thought it happened because of all the pills my psychiatrist had me popping. The antidepressants, the antipsychotics.... But then that new voice inside me told me, 'You've absorbed the power of the bug. This is your calling. This is your gift.'"

"I suppose you could call it a gift," Cliff said. He felt like this discovery should excite him due to his involvement with research on nest people. But he could only think about being trapped in this house.

"You've done the favor for me," Nathaniel said, lifting his robe back over his shoulders. "You've confirmed my destiny. And now you can go."

Thrilled, Cliff shot up from the chair, his arm bumping against the lamp's hot bulb. He steadied the lamp and asked, "I can really leave?" He glanced at Rufus, and he was able to see the man nod.

"Now if you want," Nathaniel said, "or in the morning."

"Now," Cliff said. "If you can just take me to Waverley."

Nathaniel shook his head and sighed. "Oh, no," he said, sounding grave. "Waverly won't be leaving us."

"Are you going to give me the key to the car?" Cliff asked after Rufus brought him back to his room.

"The key's already in the car," Rufus said. "Under the floor mat. I'm going to show you to the vehicle. Get your Hazard Wrap back on and get ready to go." He handed Cliff the lit candle he'd been carrying. "I'll come for you in 10."

Cliff watched Rufus pull the door closed. He didn't hear the sound of the lock. He guessed 10 minutes probably wouldn't be enough time to find Waverley, but he felt like he should try. He could at least check nearby rooms and then return to his own room and get dressed. He recalled what Nathaniel had said when he asked why Waverley couldn't leave with him: "It became clear to me she's one of the girls."

He was relieved the door swung open for him. Rufus had left the hallway, which was dark except for a few rays of moonlight entering through the window near the stairwell. He figured Rufus had returned to whatever room he stayed in to gear up for the outdoors.

Cliff crept along the hallway in the opposite direction of the stairwell. Holding the candle in front of him, he noticed a row of framed city maps on one wall. *TACOMA 1900* was printed at the bottom of the first map. The images of streets, buildings, and parks multiplied as the years of the maps increased from 1935 to 1960 to 1985 to 2015. The frame of the last map was cracked and covered in some brownish-yellow substance. Cliff frowned as he saw a wad of something in the center of the ruined map. Holding the candle closer, he recognized the smashed body of a redbug.

To the right of the last map was a door.

Cliff saw words painted on the door's surface. He had to step back to read them:

THE SON
ALWAYS
KNOWS
THE SINS
OF THE
FATHER

Cliff supposed Waverley wouldn't be inside that room, but he couldn't resist trying the doorknob.

The door opened to what appeared to be an office. The wide, many-paned window opposite Cliff framed a full moon, which cast a blue light on the room's furnishings: the massive desk in front of him, the high-backed chair tucked beneath that desk, the filled bookshelves lining the wood-paneled walls, the leather couch to the right of the desk.

The room smelled strongly of leather, but there was an underlying scent of something rancid. As Cliff stepped toward the desk, the mysterious stench grew more potent.

The candlelight showed the layer of dried blood covering the desk's surface. He glanced around the room, holding the candle before him as he sought another article of clothing nailed to a wall or a smashed picture. What he noticed was equally unsettling.

Holes throughout the couch's cushions, as if someone had stabbed the furniture dozens of times. Small white feathers protruded from the punctured areas.

Cliff checked the carpet near the couch for a knife or some other clue as to what atrocity had occurred in here.

And that was when he saw the head in the wastebasket.

His skin crawling, Cliff shuffled away from the container, which was beside the desk. His curiosity was greater than his fear, however, and he soon held the candle over the hideous object.

The head was wrapped in a clear plastic bag you'd find in the produce section of a grocery store. The silver patches of hair on either side of the grayish head showed it had belonged to a man in his late fifties or early sixties. The lips were curved downwards in a frown, and the blue eyes were open and staring up through the ceiling.

As if he were watching his son, Cliff thought.

With a shudder, he imagined Nathaniel hacking off his own father's head on that desk. He suddenly doubted Nathaniel was really going to free him. Why should he trust a lunatic who had most likely murdered his father and stepmother?

Cliff rushed out of the office, and his quick movement extinguished the candle's flame. Once in the black hallway again, he knew he wouldn't be able to find Waverley. He needed to leave the house now. He remembered the plane he'd heard earlier. If he could locate his rescuers, he'd be able to point them to the mansion and they could extract Waverley and "the girls."

He was about to enter his room and fetch his Hazard Wrap when he heard footsteps in the stairwell. He ran to the end of the hallway and hid behind a large vase that was between the doorway to the stairwell and the window. He felt a droplet of sweat descend from his temple.

Rufus stepped out of the stairwell and started toward Cliff's room. He wore the exterminator uniform he'd had on earlier in the day. Cliff didn't wait for Rufus to reach the door. He dropped the candle and tore into the stairwell. He descended as quickly and quietly as possible.

His flight took him into the mansion's foyer, and he collided with the statue of the winged horse. He watched with terror as the statue tipped over and crashed loudly on the tiled floor. One of its wings broke off and slid into a corner.

Cliff glanced back at the darkness of the stairwell, expecting to see Rufus emerge. No one showed. After unlocking the front door, he ran down the front stairs that would deliver him to the driveway. He was grateful to feel the brisk night air. He was nervous about a redbug landing on his skin, but he was more afraid of Rufus or Nathaniel catching up to him. He figured he could find refuge in a house somewhere and assemble a protective covering out of someone's abandoned wardrobe.

Or maybe he'd run into his rescuers.

Thankfully, the front yard was dark enough to conceal his passage. The only light came from an electric lantern hanging from the ceiling of the distant gazebo. Cliff paused on the driveway when he saw a shadowy group of people standing on the grass near the gazebo. His eyes widened.

One woman had a protruding belly that showed her pregnancy. Next to her was a woman holding hands with two little girls.

Cliff stared at the pregnant woman, whose short black hair and long pale neck made her resemble Viola. He could almost believe she was Viola if he hadn't seen his girlfriend's crumpled, lifeless body lying in the ivy bed in front of Harborview.

He glanced back and saw the front door of the house remained closed. Rather than head toward the estate's gate, he hurried across the overgrown lawn in the direction of the gazebo.

The woman standing between the two little girls was Rachel. She wore her maid's uniform while the pregnant woman had on an ankle-length black dress. As Cliff approached, each of the children hid behind one of the women. He guessed both of the little girls were nest people.

"I'm leaving now," he told the group in that steady, authoritative voice he'd used whenever he addressed research participants at Harborview. "I think all of you should leave with me. This is no place for children."

Rachel reached behind her and patted the girl's arm reassuringly. Cliff was unable to see either of the girls' faces. He guessed they couldn't have been more than 5 or 6 years old.

"Please just go," Rachel said in a quiet voice. "You're putting us in danger by being here."

"I heard an airplane flying overhead today," Cliff said. "There are rescuers searching for me. They may be in the neighborhood. They can take you to a refugee center."

Rachel sneered at him. "I've spent time in one of those places. I'm never going back."

"Don't you understand that Nathaniel's insane?" Cliff realized the pointlessness of his question when he remembered he was talking to a nest person. How could Rachel truly understand? And yet he sensed she really was different from most nest people. She was cognizant.

"You're the one who doesn't understand," Rachel said, shaking her head. "We're protected here. Please leave before Nathaniel hears you."

"Are these your daughters?" Cliff asked. "You're a mother?"

Rachel was silent. She only offered him another one of her emotionless stares.

"They're Daphne's," the pregnant woman said. "She's working her shift now. She gives Nathaniel a massage every night before he sleeps, sleeps."

Cliff cringed when he imagined the woman's fingers sliding past that dead redbug beneath Nathaniel's flesh. "What's your name?" he asked the pregnant woman.

"Sheryl."

"Will you leave with me? That will be best for your baby."

"I don't think they'll let me, me."

"You mean Nathaniel and Rufus? But they're not here. We can leave now."

The woman glanced in the direction of the gazebo. Cliff frowned when he looked where she did.

Giant redbugs clung to a board beneath the gazebo's roof. The hanging electric lantern illuminated the movement of their antennae. One of the insects beat its wings.

Alarmed, Cliff remembered he was without Hazard Wrap. "I'm leaving now and I'm taking these girls with me. Sheryl, are you coming?"

Sheryl gave a confused look toward Rachel, who shook her head. Rachel reached back with both hands to hold the girl close to her.

Cliff was annoyed by her obstinacy. "You can decide about your own future," he said, "but I won't let you put these girls' lives at risk."

He moved forward and reached around Sheryl to grasp the girl's arm. "Everything's going to be all right," he told her. "I'll make sure you get to a safe place."

He withdrew his hand when he felt a burning sensation in his fingers. He stared down at the bare skin of his hand, which appeared to be turning even whiter than usual.

The girl stepped out from behind Sheryl and glared up at him.

Her eyes resembled spheres of coal. The skin of her face had a hardness to it, as if it were made of plastic. Protruding from her forehead were two red lengths of flesh—antennae.

"No!" Cliff said. His horrified voice was nearly a shout. "This isn't possible."

He stepped backwards, but something was wrong with his legs. He stumbled and fell to the ground. His hand felt like it was in the midst of flames. The pain traveled up his arm and spread throughout his torso. Sweat seeped through his skin. He wasn't able to lift any of his limbs.

He saw the girl standing over him, scowling. Rachel moved next to her and stared down at Cliff with a concerned expression.

"Please," Cliff tried to say. But he never spoke the word because his lips wouldn't move. He only exhaled.

"I'm sorry," Rachel said. "Ava didn't do it on purpose."

Cliff heard a voice coming from high above them. It belonged to Nathaniel.

"I see you, Rachel and Sheryl, and I see your little monsters. Stay there. Don't try to hide."

Cliff pictured Nathaniel on his balcony, most likely naked with crazed eyes. He tried to cry out, but he was unable to produce a sound.

Rachel and the girl disappeared from view. He heard Rachel say, "Go next door."

His eyelids felt as if they were swelling, and his vision became cloudy. His tears only made it more difficult to see. His heartbeat seemed to be faltering. As he lay on the grass, he suddenly feared that Viola was walking away from him with Rachel.

Before losing consciousness, he saw Rufus peering down at him through the scratched face shield of an exterminator helmet. He held a flashlight. Waverley appeared beside him and gazed at Cliff. She wore a maid's uniform. She didn't seem to recognize him.

"Rome has some spooky statues," she said. She put her arm around Rufus's shoulder. "When can we take the train to Naples, Dad? I'm ready to see the volcano."

2. RACHEL JENSEN

"Go next door," Rachel repeated to Sheryl. "Hide the girls. I'll get there as soon as I can." She watched Sheryl lead Daphne's daughters through the trees toward the green mansion with the pillars in front. The mansion where Daphne had given birth to Ava and June just last month. The mansion where Rachel had given birth to Carlotta on that snowy morning in January.

Where was she? Carlotta usually came to them during their walks at night, emerging cat-like from a bush or even climbing down from the roof of the gazebo. But tonight she hadn't appeared.

Instead, that poor man had interrupted them. He lay in the grass, his body shaking from a seizure. Rachel watched him from behind a tree trunk. Carlos's body had jerked like that before he died on her bed in Mirror Lake. Rachel placed pillows around his head so he wouldn't knock it against the wall and she held his hand until it went stiff and he let out a long, raspy sigh.

Rufus and the tall blonde girl just stood over that man's body, staring down at him.

Rachel felt like she owed him something. After all, he hadn't told Nathaniel she truly was different from the others. She'd often feared Nathaniel would realize she didn't have the obedient, robot-like minds of Miyoko and Heather. Or she was more conscious than Sheryl. Or her thoughts had stopped loop loop looping because the bug inside her had died.

Each morning she put cover-up on the welt over that bug so the insect looked less gray.

But Rachel supposed the dead bug wasn't the main reason she could think more clearly. It was because she was the mother of a growing girl.

An unusual girl.

A girl she needed to find and care for.

When the man's body went limp in the grass she hurried toward the side of the house Carlotta often climbed after dark.

Rachel stared up at the fourth floor from the brick pathway that ran alongside the house. Seeing that Nathaniel's bedroom was unlit, she worried about Daphne, who'd been giving Nathaniel a massage at the time of the commotion on the front lawn. Daphne was her friend and the only other nest person who had a mind as uncluttered as hers.

Like Rachel, Daphne had become more coherent the longer she was a mother. The bug under the skin of her shoulder only squirmed a little when you pressed your finger against it.

Daphne hadn't been on the balcony when Nathaniel yelled down at them. What if Nathaniel had harmed her because he somehow knew the girls were hers?

Rachel didn't think he'd ever seen the children before. She and the others were so careful about keeping them in the attic of the pool house during the day. She and Sheryl and Daphne took them on strolls only at night, from the pool house to the gazebo to the mansion next door, where they played old board games Daphne had found in the dead neighbor woman's closet. Sometimes they dressed up in the dead woman's gowns and furs.

Carlotta never played with them because she was growing rapidly. Four months old and she looked like she was 12 years old. She wanted to do other things. Strange things, like peer at Nathaniel through his bedroom window.

Nathaniel seemed to be aware that someone was watching him, but he'd never seen Carlotta before.

"There was a being outside my window last night," he'd told Rachel last week while she positioned his mirror on the deck. "I could feel its presence."

She gave him that blank-faced look she'd learned by watching other nest people in the refugee center.

"The beings want to drag me down into my grave because they know I'll be rising soon." Nathaniel pulled her closer to him and pointed at the mirror, which offered a blinding reflection of the sun.

Rachel squinted.

"That's what the future's going to look like when I'm at the center of it. I'm going to burn through all the beings that shouldn't be here."

Rachel now stared up at the shaded stretch of chimney that rose past Nathaniel's bedroom window. Carlotta often clung to the chimney, watching Nathaniel even though Rachel had warned her against it.

Rachel wondered if Carlotta wanted a masculine figure in her life because all she had was her mother.

And the bugs.

Rachel decided Carlotta wasn't on the side of the house. She was about to start toward the backyard when she noticed a few of the larger insects clinging to a branch near her head. Seeing the bugs gave her skin a cold, prickly feeling even though she'd sensed they could no longer poison her. She suspected they could still harm her if they wanted. And there was something disapproving in the way they watched her now. As if they were angry about her losing track of her daughter.

Heading to the pool house, Rachel recalled that morning Carlotta came out of her. The four-and-a-half-month pregnancy had been relatively easy. She had no nausea or vomiting, and her stomach only ballooned about a month before she gave birth. But her innards felt like they were on fire as Carlotta made her way into the world.

Sheryl helped with the birthing process, which spanned half a day in an upstairs bedroom of the green mansion. At one point, Rachel asked Sheryl for a wooden spoon to put in her mouth so she wouldn't accidentally bite through her lip or cheeks while pushing the baby out of her. As Carlotta emerged, Rachel moaned loudly. She turned her head and saw snow falling outside the window. She felt as if her spirit was going to evacuate her body and journey upward into the white sky, but then the burning and the pain suddenly stopped.

She heard a baby's gurgle before she lost consciousness.

"Would you like to hold your daughter? Your daughter?" Sheryl asked when Rachel awoke.

Rachel sat up in bed, eager to see the baby.

The baby that Sheryl carried from the dim corner of the room.

The baby with solidly black eyes and bumps on its red forehead resembling the nubs of horns.

The baby that couldn't have been her and Carlos's child.

"Take it away from me," she said, shaking her head and shrinking against the pillows on the bed. "I can't look at it."

But as Sheryl moved away from the mattress the baby actually reached for Rachel with two tiny, chubby arms. Rachel's heartbeat quickened when she heard what sounded like "Mama."

She knew Carlotta was hers.

Rachel became hopeful when she saw the silhouette of a female figure standing in the doorway of the pool house. She ran past the pool, ready to embrace her daughter.

"Carlotta?" she called in a recklessly loud voice.

As she neared the house, a flickering candle behind the figure showed she was too wide and too tall to be Carlotta. She was a woman rather than a girl, and she wore a maid's uniform.

Daphne.

"You're okay," Rachel said to her distraught-looking friend. She concealed her disappointment at not finding her daughter. She hugged Daphne. She used to think of her as the mannequin with the light brown bangs and the bright red lipstick. Daphne would always be at Rufus's side or just a few paces behind him. But then after Daphne became pregnant she shook off Rufus and gained humanness.

Daphne gently pulled away from her and looked at her with tearing eyes. "I had to tell him. Nathaniel said he'd kill the girls and all of you if I didn't."

"What'd you say?"

"Where they are. I told him about how we go to the house next door." Daphne's eyeliner bled darkly down her cheeks.

"Did you tell him about Carlotta?" Rachel said in a nervous voice.

"No. He even asked if you were the mother of the 'little monsters' he saw in the front yard. I told him the twins were mine and they're not little monsters. They're just...unique."

Daphne continued to weep, and Rachel held her.

"I do love them," Daphne whispered.

"Of course you do. You're their mother." She remembered cradling Baby Ava while Daphne had struggled to breastfeed Baby June. "Your milk is going to be orange-ish and thick like that," she'd consoled Daphne, "and there's going to be little of it. They don't need much milk, and they grow like sponges in water."

She stopped hugging Daphne and led her inside the pool house. She glanced behind her to look for Nathaniel. She only saw the black water of the pool and the dark garden.

Upon shutting the door, she hollered, "Carlotta?" She knew it was unlikely she'd hear a reply. Carlotta had stopped sleeping in the attic a month ago, when she lost her little girl looks and her need to cling to her mother. She became an adolescent with lanky limbs, wispy antennae, and unreadable eyes that studied you more than they watched you.

Rachel no longer knew where her daughter slept.

"Nobody's here but us," Daphne said.

Rachel nodded, but she picked up the burning candle from the living room shelf and inspected the house anyway. She climbed the ladder to the attic and glanced around the small space with the slanted ceiling. She only saw little piles of Daphne's daughters' clothes and the two wool blankets that served as the girls' bedding.

She then checked the house's one bedroom. The twin beds were empty. The made bed was the one where Veronique had died after the bug crawled out of her neck a couple months ago. The bed with the rumpled covers was where Sheryl had slept since her pregnancy began to show.

"Did you tell Nathaniel about Rufus?" Rachel turned to Daphne, whose face was a mess from the smeared make-up.

"He didn't ask who the father was. He just said, 'I'll bet Rufus knows about the little monsters.'"

Rachel nodded. She'd once asked Daphne if Rufus had forced her to have sex.

"I didn't mind when he'd come to my room," Daphne had said. "He has a way of making you feel like you're the most special girl in the world and he'll protect you against everything that's going wrong. And there's a lot going wrong."

But then after Daphne was pregnant and staying in the pool house Rufus must have made Sheryl feel like she was the most special girl in the world.

"I need to find Carlotta," Rachel said, handing Daphne the candle. "I'll come for you and your girls after I find her."

"Nathaniel's going to hold a meeting in the ballroom. He wanted me to tell everyone."

"I won't be going to anymore meetings," Rachel said.

During the five months she'd been here, she'd known she couldn't leave until Carlotta was old enough. She'd had reasons to go. Nathaniel was beyond mentally ill, and Rufus was someone she didn't fully trust. She'd heard the others' morbid stories about what was inside some of the house's "forbidden" rooms. Other guests who'd stayed at the mansion—a business partner of Nathaniel's father, a trio of exterminators—disappeared. There were also supposed to be two corpses on the beach.

But the mansion had offered Rachel and Carlotta shelter, food, and safety—or at least the semblance of safety.

Until now.

"I don't know what's going to happen here," Rachel told Daphne. "I think things are going to get much worse." She squeezed her friend's hand and then opened the front door.

She froze when she saw Rufus standing outside with a look of despair beyond his face shield.

"You're both wanted in the house," he said.

Rachel had never heard Rufus say so much at one time.

"You said you'd keep them hidden," he told Daphne as the three of them approached the mansion. He gripped her arm by the pool. "That was the deal. You keep them hidden or you get rid of them. I can tell you Nathaniel will get rid of them."

"Nathaniel said he wouldn't hurt them." Daphne sounded as if she would start crying again. "He promised me upstairs in his bedroom."

"And you believe that promise?"

"More than I believe any of yours. Tell me, Rufus, is that new blonde girl going to be your next one?"

Rachel glanced at Rufus, but she couldn't see his reaction in the dark.

"Where are my girls now?" Daphne asked, her voice weakening. "Did you bring them over from next door?"

Rufus remained silent. He opened one of the French doors and waited for Daphne and Rachel to enter the living room.

Rachel paused when she heard the plane flying above the house. She glanced up and spotted a blinking red light in the starry sky. She'd seen a plane around sunset. The same kind of plane had flown over the forest months ago while she lay in those ferns, waiting for Tess to find her. She finally decided to leave the "antidote" in the ferns and get out of the forest on her own. She figured that Tess, though kindhearted, would only lead her to more government workers who would stick her in a refugee center and eventually separate her from her baby.

She'd already been separated from too many people in her life.

She glanced around the garden, hoping to see Carlotta crouched by a hedge or among the rows of tulips.

"Inside," Rufus said.

Rachel almost asked him if he'd seen her daughter.

They moved from the living room to the front hallway. Rachel noticed that the marble horse statue lay on its side. One of its front legs was missing. Nathaniel had once pointed at that horse and told her, "When I ascend, a chariot could take me, or I may rise on my own."

"Upstairs," Rufus instructed the women, pointing into the stairwell.

When they entered the ballroom, Rachel saw all the chandeliers were lit. Someone had painted the word *KING* in the centers of the gold-framed mirrors lining the walls.

Nathaniel stood at the other end of the ballroom with Daphne's daughters beside him. He still wore his robe. Also present were the rest of "the girls": Miyoko, Heather, and a grim-faced Sheryl. The blonde girl was among the group. She had a dazed expression on her face. Her maid's uniform looked too tight.

Rachel was grateful Carlotta wasn't there.

"Welcome, welcome," Nathaniel called to the newly arrived trio. He beckoned for them to join the group.

As they neared, Rachel saw Rufus remove his exterminator helmet and unzip the top part of his uniform. He looked exhausted, and his forehead was covered in sweat. She remembered how he'd kindly wrapped a quilt around her shivering body when she first arrived at the house in December.

"You can have your baby in the house next door and you're welcome to stay with us," he'd told her. "But you can't ever let Nathaniel know you're pregnant and he can't ever see your child."

Rachel now considered offering him some consoling words, but she had nothing to say.

"Everyone gather in a circle, circle," Nathaniel said. "Except for you two," he told Daphne's daughters. "You stay by me." The girls continually watched their mother.

Rachel saw Daphne was crying again.

"I'd like to talk about how you make a baby," Nathaniel told the group, his eyes blinking. "How you make a baby. Or a little monster, monster."

Daphne released a loud sob, and Rachel patted her back.

"Don't you touch her!" Nathaniel said. "I'll have nobody feeling sorry for a maker of monsters."

"You said you wouldn't harm them," Daphne spoke up, wiping away her tears with the back of her hand.

Rachel glanced around at the others, most of whom showed a mix of confusion and fear.

"Do you see me harming anyone?" Nathaniel asked. "I'm just bringing these girls together with their makers. Because you see it takes more than one, one. You have a mommy monster maker and a daddy monster maker. A mommy and a daddy, a mommy and a daddy."

Rachel snuck a glance at Rufus, who stared at the ballroom floor. One corner of his mouth was twitching.

"I didn't make these girls with you," Nathaniel told Daphne, "because I know what happens with little monsters, monsters. They grow into big monsters that kill their makers and prevent them from reaching their highest destinies, destinies. So that means if I'm not the monsters' daddy then someone else is."

"Nathaniel," Rufus said.

"No," Nathaniel snapped. Despite the forcefulness of his voice, it betrayed his pain. "You don't get to speak anymore."

Rufus looked downwards once again.

"Bring him in!" Nathaniel shouted. His eyes were on the entrance to the ballroom.

Rachel glanced behind her and saw a man with a wrestler's mask and goggles and protective suit made of garbage bags. The man who'd used a crowbar to smash the window of the abandoned car in which she slept months ago. The man who forced her to the mansion's front gate and waited with her until Rufus appeared in the driveway.

Rachel had never seen the man since that winter's day. Today he entered the ballroom with something dragging behind him.

The corpse of the man who'd died on the front lawn.

Like most people who'd been exposed to redbug toxin, the dead man appeared to be severely burned. His eyes were partly open, and yellowed. His hands were in the shapes of claws, just as Carlos's had been when Rachel buried him and her sister in the backyard. A wide smear of dirt was on the front of his sweater.

Rachel turned to the blonde girl to see her reaction, but the girl looked as if she were still lost in a daydream.

The man in the wrestler's mask slid the corpse into the center of the circle. "This is the second time I'm delivering him to you today," he joked. "Aren't you impressed I scared him and the blondie into coming here this morning?"

"You can go now," Nathaniel said.

"I found the one you saw on the gazebo roof," the man said. "She was hiding in the trees."

Rachel's eyes grew large, and a look of panic replaced the sedate expression she tried to maintain at all times.

"But I lost her," the man continued. "She ran off in the direction of the water. I think I shot her in the shoulder, though."

"My baby," Rachel murmured. She repeatedly shook her head. Tears stung her eyes. She backed away from the circle. She considered the fastest way to get out of the house and into the backyard. She was turning to run toward the doorway when Nathaniel said, "Grab her! Lock this other mommy in the coat closet."

Rufus immediately responded to Nathaniel's order. He took hold of Rachel's arm and yanked her toward the closet, a wide space with two sliding doors. He opened one of the doors and pushed her inside. Her head collided with coat hangers, and she fell to the cold wooden floor. She scrambled to rise and run past Rufus, but he slid the door shut and locked it before she could escape.

Behind her was a circular window facing the front yard. Rachel considered getting out through that window, but it had no latch. And there was a two-story drop to the ground.

The closet doors wouldn't budge when she tried forcing them open.

She stood on her toes to look through one of the glass panels that ran the length of the sliding doors. She watched Rufus walk back toward the others.

"Go now," Nathaniel told the man in the wrestler's mask. "I'll pay you later, later."

As the man left the ballroom, Rachel dreaded him stalking Carlotta, who was wounded and bleeding somewhere out there in the night. She tried to hold back her tears.

"In this house," Nathaniel told the circle, "we've got more than one mommy. And obviously we've got a daddy, a daddy. And together they've made little monsters that can turn a man into this." He pointed at the corpse, and then he placed his hand on one of Daphne's daughters' shoulders. "But what I'm really wondering about is if the monsters' daddy is immune to their poison."

"Nathaniel," Rufus said, "I-"

"You're nothing to me, me," Nathaniel said, his voice cracking. "As far as I'm concerned, you're what my stepmom thought of you—a sad ex-chemical soldier who cleans rich people's pools."

"Don't let this ruin everything," Rufus said.

"Nothing's ruined, ruined, ruined." Nathaniel shook his head violently, as if he were trying to free a thought from his skull. He stared at Rufus. "I have my destiny, and you have your monster family."

Rachel frowned as she watched Nathaniel bring one of Daphne's daughters—June—toward Rufus. The girl looked terrified.

"I want you to give your daddy a kiss on the cheek," Nathaniel told the girl.

Daphne whimpered.

"Kneel so your daughter can give you that kiss," Nathaniel told Rufus.

Rufus shook his head. "Nathaniel, please." Even from the coat closet, Rachel could see the sweat on his brow.

"So you won't do this for me, me?" Nathaniel asked.

"Nathaniel. I won't. You and I-"

"Judas!" Nathaniel shrieked. He withdrew a knife from his pocket and plunged it into Rufus's gut. He wrenched it free and stabbed again and again, mutilating the man. "Judas, Judas, Judas!"

June stepped away from Nathaniel, and the horrified circle of nest people broke apart.

Rachel watched Rufus collapse to his knees, blood spilling down his thighs and pooling onto the ballroom floor. Nathaniel continued to thrust the knife into him even after he toppled over onto the corpse.

"Daphne!" Rachel shouted from the closet.

Daphne turned toward her like a frightened deer. Fortunately, Nathaniel didn't seem to hear her. He appeared to be in a murderous daze. Rachel pointed at the doorway, signaling for Daphne to get out of the ballroom.

When she saw Daphne collecting her girls, Rachel went to the closet's circular window. She knew it was a dangerous drop to the front yard, but she guessed Nathaniel would kill her if she stayed here. She lifted a table from one end of the closet and smashed it against the window. Glass shattered. She scrambled onto the table and squeezed through the window, a shard of glass slicing her hip.

She fell arms first through a rhododendron tree. Something snapped in her left wrist when she hit dirt. She cried out from the pain. After catching her breath, she lifted herself up and tucked her hurt wrist under her arm. She checked her wounded hip with her other hand. Luckily, she was only slightly bleeding. She started toward one side of the house.

As she fled, she glanced up at the ballroom window. She recognized the silhouettes of the large redbugs that were always around the yard. The insects clung to the glass. She'd first noticed those insects when she arrived in winter. They had pressed against the neighboring mansion's windows following Carlotta's birth.

Rachel was wondering about the location of her daughter when someone tripped her in the driveway. Her sprained wrist hit the cement, and she cried out as the pain shot up to her shoulder. Her attacker yanked her by the hair and forced her to look at him.

Moonlight showed the man in the wrestler's mask staring down at her. He held a shotgun.

"So you thought you'd get away, bitch?"

Rachel didn't answer.

"Were you hoping those rescue men would help you? Sorry. Those men came and went. They landed their plane on the golf course, they sniffed around that Humvee and those dead exterminators I shot up, and then they took off. So much for Homeland Security, eh, sweetheart?"

Rachel only glared at him. She wished she'd searched for some kind of weapon in the coat closet or front yard.

The man pulled her by the hair toward the house, and she whimpered. Her wrist was radiating pain.

"I'll bet Nathaniel will pay double for you. Sometimes I think I should keep one of you ladies for my own fun. But you're not exactly a real lady anymore, and I don't want a cockroach carrier sharing my bed."

Rachel stopped resisting and walked willingly toward the front door of the house. The man released her hair. He moved closely behind her and gave her an occasional shove. Though she dreaded seeing Nathaniel again, she was relieved she was distracting this man from his hunt for her daughter.

The front door swung open before Rachel could place her hand on the doorknob.

Daphne and her girls stood in the candlelit foyer. They were obviously shocked to see Rachel and the man shadowing her. They stepped back from the doorway.

"Well, if it isn't freak mama and her two mutants," the man said. "Time for you all to turn around and march back upstairs." He grabbed Rachel by the hair again and pulled her inside the hallway. She grimaced.

"Aunt Rachel?" one of the girls asked. It was Ava. "He's hurting you."

"It'll be okay, sweetie," Rachel muttered, knowing it wouldn't be.

"He's hurting you," Ava repeated, scowling. She approached Rachel.

"Don't come closer." The man locked an arm around Rachel's neck. He pressed the gun's barrel against her temple.

"Ava, stop," Daphne said in a pleading voice.

The girl took another step forward.

Rachel felt the man's body stiffen. She lifted one foot and kicked her heel against his calf.

"Cunt!" the man hissed, losing his grip on her. Rachel reeled around and tried to grab the gun with her uninjured hand. The man stumbled against the wall by the door but kept his fingers around the gun's handle. Rachel slammed her body against his in her effort to free the weapon. During their struggle, the man's garbage bag sleeve ripped and his arm became exposed.

"Leave Aunt Rachel alone!" Ava screamed. She took hold of the man's forearm, and he howled before dropping the gun.

He glanced down at his arm as if something had bitten it, and then he looked at the young girl with horror before sinking to the floor. His body began to shake from seizures.

"We need to get out of the house," Rachel told Daphne and her daughters. She retrieved the man's gun from the floor and handed it to Daphne. She led them through the door with an eye on Ava, who showed no emotion. She wondered if this quickly growing girl understood the lethal power of her touch.

Rachel closed the door to block out the sight of the stricken man and the awful wheezing sound coming from between his frozen lips.

"Where's Nathaniel?" she asked Daphne.

"He was in the ballroom when we left. He was still stab- He was still with Rufus." Daphne gazed mournfully down the steps. "Where will we go?"

"You'll go to that yellow house two blocks from here."

Rachel and Daphne had taken the girls there the evening after Veronique died. Their depression gave them a reckless wanderlust. They found an unopened bag of Halloween candy in the pantry, and they sat around the dining room table in silence, eating the sweets while a candle burned on the table.

"If we live through this," Daphne had said that night, "where do you want to end up?"

"Back in Mirror Lake," Rachel said without hesitating. "I know I'll go there when Carlotta's old enough."

Now she didn't even know if Carlotta was alive. She started down the stairs, and Daphne and the girls followed. She hugged the three of them in the driveway.

"We'll wait for you in the yellow house," Daphne said. "And we won't come back here again."

Rachel nodded and said, "No. Never again."

While sneaking into the backyard, Rachel noticed that the mansion's lights began to blink on. She hid behind the pool house and folded her arms so her hurt wrist was in the warmth of her armpit. The pain was easing a little. She watched the growing illumination, wondering if Nathaniel was about to come out of the house in pursuit of her.

Nathaniel and Rufus had always been conservative with the electricity to preserve the generator, but now rooms on all four floors of the house glowed yellow.

All the bedrooms of "the girls" on the third floor.

The second-floor TV room where Nathaniel had painted over the flat-screen TV one of the "messages" he received: *THE HIGHEST MOUNTAINTOP SHALL BE LOWER THAN ME.*

The living room on the ground floor. Rachel saw Miyoko walk through that room and open one of the French doors. She left the house and started moving chairs away from the area just beside the doorway.

Rachel was reluctant about approaching. Nathaniel would be able to see her if she came into the light, and she needed to reach Carlotta. But she also wanted to warn Miyoko about staying in the house.

She looked at the upper floors to check for Nathaniel. He wasn't visible in any of the windows. Someone moved on the third-floor balcony directly above where Miyoko was doing her clearing. Rachel recognized Heather's close-cropped haircut. Heather was tying rope around the balustrade.

"Miyoko," Rachel whispered. She stepped out of the shadows of the pool house.

Miyoko turned to her with a potted cactus in her arms. As she looked at Rachel, she showed no emotion. Miyoko and Heather were the least conscious and most obedient of Nathaniel's "girls." Rachel had often tried to imagine the two women working in their past professions. Miyoko had been a dentist—Nathaniel's dentist, actually—and Heather had owned a used bookstore in Gig Harbor.

Miyoko smiled widely at Rachel. "Nathaniel's looking for you," she said. She set the cactus near the edge of the swimming pool.

"Please whisper," Rachel said. She glanced up at the balcony again, and she spotted the new blonde girl peering down at them. "You and Heather need to leave this house. All of you need to get out. Where's Sheryl?"

Miyoko shrugged. Rachel was relieved the pregnant woman might have escaped.

"Please leave," Rachel said. "I don't know what Nathaniel's going to do, but-"

"Nathaniel rises tonight," Miyoko whispered, smiling again. "That's why we're preparing just as he told us. Nathaniel's looking for you. He said he needs to find you and then he rises."

Rachel stepped backwards, nervous Miyoko would try to grab her.

"We're preparing just as he told us," Miyoko repeated, looking around the area she'd been clearing. "Nathaniel rises tonight. Our work will be done here." She entered the living room and disappeared into the foyer.

Rachel looked up at the balcony again. Heather was tying another piece of rope around the balustrade. Rachel guessed the rope was part of one of those crazy tasks Nathaniel had his "girls" perform for him. Maybe he thought his chariot was going to deliver into the sky not just him but his entire mansion.

"Have you seen my dad?"

Rachel saw the blonde girl standing by the balustrade with her hands clasped together. She stared down at Rachel.

"I lost him at the Spanish Steps," she said. "Do you speak English? Parlare inglese? Parlare inglese?"

Rachel shook her head in frustration. She decided to grab the electric lantern off the table by the pool and finally find Carlotta. As she started across the garden in the direction of the beach, she heard Miyoko's voice behind her.

"Nathaniel rises tonight!"

Rachel looked back to see Miyoko on the balcony with Heather and the blonde girl. Miyoko and Heather helped the blonde girl straddle the balustrade. She then moved out of the straddling position so she sat on the balustrade and her feet dangled far above the area Miyoko had cleared. Soon all three women sat on the balustrade.

Rachel realized each one had a piece of rope encircling her neck.

"Oh, no." She was about to run back toward the house when the blonde girl fell from the balcony. Rachel turned away so she wouldn't witness the girl's neck break. When she looked back, she saw the dead girl's body gently swaying just above the ground.

Heather was next.

"Nathaniel rises tonight!" Miyoko called before she shoved herself off the balustrade. Her body plummeted with her legs straight and her arms at her sides, as if she were jumping into a lake.

Rachel placed her hand over her tearing eyes. She ran away in the direction of the beach.

The sound of a plane made Rachel look upwards. She couldn't see its lights, but she heard its engine grow louder as it passed over the property.

Maybe the rescue team was returning. The thought didn't encourage her. She imagined presenting Carlotta to a semi-circle of Homeland Security workers who would most likely gawk at her daughter's insect features and take samples of her exoskeletal skin before stealing her away to some experimentation center.

Rachel would get Carlotta to Mirror Lake without the government's help. They would drive or walk, but they'd never receive rides from exterminators. They'd sleep in empty houses and not in refugee centers. The weather would be warming up in eastern Washington by now. They could sit in the sun near Carlos's grave and decide how they'd like their lives to be.

Once the plane passed, Rachel heard the Puget Sound's water lapping the shore. The moon cast a bluish light on the evergreens bordering the steep, rocky incline that turned into the beach. Jutting from the middle of the shore was a pier leading to a rowboat.

"Carlotta?" Rachel called as she descended the incline in the direction of the pier. She imagined her daughter lying on the floor of the boat, in pain and weeping—although she hadn't seen Carlotta cry in over a month, when her daughter had asked, "If the twins' daddy lives in the house, then where does mine live?"

Rachel tripped on a rock and her injured wrist slammed against a stone. She howled from the pain. Crouching on the rocks, she searched for the switch on the electric lantern. Although she feared Nathaniel spotting the light, she needed the lantern on to navigate this treacherous beach.

The lantern cast a circle of light around her. Rachel noticed the rocks grew smoother the closer they were to the water. On the edge of the circle of light was what resembled a massive tangle of seaweed. Rachel lifted the lantern to increase the light's reach, and she immediately regretting doing so.

What she'd thought was seaweed was actually a pair of decayed, naked corpses bound together with wire.

Rachel couldn't see the faces. She saw the back of a woman's head, her tangled blonde hair holding leaves and other debris. The accompanying corpse was decapitated. Rachel thought she spotted tattered cash beneath the wire.

She lowered the lantern so she could no longer view the bodies. She remembered Daphne telling her of the two corpses on the beach. Daphne had found them while walking with the girls. Rachel had told her she wouldn't go to the beach. She'd seen enough death before coming to the mansion. She wanted to focus on life.

"Mama?"

Rachel bolted upright from her seated position. "Carlotta?" she called in her loudest voice. She thrust out the lantern in various directions. "Where are you, baby?"

"In here, Mama."

The voice came from the incline. As she moved across the rocks, Rachel saw there was a break in the incline where two rusty metal doors protruded.

She approached the doorway with the electric lantern held out before her. She thought she saw a hand pressing against one of the doors, but as she neared she realized the hand was actually one of the large redbugs. The bug skittered to the top of the door and lifted into the night sky.

"Baby?" Rachel called.

"In here, Mama."

The lantern's light revealed that the space in the incline was filled with redbug egg sacs. The orange, glistening sacs lined the walls and hung from the ceiling in thick, tubular clumps. Rachel could see the brown, spherical eggs inside the sacs. The large red-bugs speckled the network of nests, their feelers rising whenever the lantern cast its light on them.

Rachel couldn't see her daughter. "Carlotta!" she said in a panicked voice.

"Come inside, Mama."

Rachel had to squeeze between the sticky sacs to reach the rear of the space. She guessed it was some kind of storage closet or bunker. She held the lantern near her chest, and sometimes the light showed a redbug retreating upwards toward the ceiling. Though she feared the insects, she mostly resented them right now. The countless eggs proved the redbug family was strong and ever multiplying.

Meanwhile, Rachel only had Carlotta left. Her parents' corpses lay in body bags in a gym in Mirror Lake. Her brother and youngest sister had most likely died near her sister's summer camp in Idaho. Her sister Beth was buried next to Carlos. During her hitchhiking to Seattle, she'd borrowed a couple's cell phone to call a refugee center and ask if her sister Melanie was registered in the system. The woman said she was unable to locate that name.

"Mama!"

Rachel peered into the darkness and finally spotted her daughter's face. As Carlotta smiled at her, Rachel thought she had the same mouth as Carlos. Rachel pushed past egg sacs to hug her daughter, and she saw Carlotta's body was coated in the jelly-like substance that made up the sacs. Carlotta wore the yellow tank top and thin athletic pants Rachel had found for her in the house next door. One of the insects rested on her left shoulder, and another was on her stomach.

Rachel tried not to show her aversion to the insects as she embraced her daughter. "Were you shot, baby?" she asked. She held up the lantern to get a better view of her.

Her daughter stroked the redbug on her stomach. "They've been taking care of me, Mama. I feel better already."

Rachel forced a smile. She was sure Carlotta was correct. The redbugs had a way of protecting when they wanted. She remembered how they'd waited nearby, sentinel-like, during the births of Carlotta and Daphne's daughters.

"Let me see your wound," Rachel said.

Carlotta turned to show her bare right shoulder. What should have been red and bleeding profusely looked pink and scabbing beneath the egg sac substance.

"Did you get hurt, too?" Carlotta asked, staring at her mother's limp left hand.

"Just my wrist," Rachel said in a dismissive voice.

"This will help." Carlotta scooped some of the orange substance covering her upper chest and slathered it on her mother's wrist.

Rachel was frightened when she felt the goo binding to her skin, but then a comforting, tingling sensation spread from her wrist through her entire arm.

"I wanted to come off the roof and be with you, Mama," Carlotta said. "But there was that man shaking on the ground, and the man who you said must never see me."

"That's all right, Baby," Rachel said.

"What happened to the man on the ground? Is that what death is?"

"That's how it can be."

"Is that how it was for my father?"

Rachel sighed. She remembered using her fingers to close Carlos's eyes after he'd passed and wrapping him in her floral bed sheet. She'd said a prayer for him.

May you walk in beauty once you reach the land of the dead.

"Your father's death was similar to that," she told Carlotta.

"I don't like it."

Rachel hugged her again. "Neither do I," she said. She peered into her daughter's black eyes. "Baby, it's time for us to leave this place. We're no longer safe here."

Surprisingly, Carlotta gave a knowing nod. "They told me I would be going soon."

"'They'?" Rachel asked even though she intuited her daughter was referring to the redbugs.

Carlotta gently pressed her hand against the insect on her stomach and said in an affectionate voice, "Them."

Of course, Rachel knew her daughter had a connection with the insects. How could she not with redbug DNA most likely being part of her DNA? Nest people also had a certain closeness with the insects that was more than physical. During her pregnancy, Rachel had always sensed where she would be safest, as if she'd developed some internal, protective compass. But Nathaniel was the only one who'd claimed redbugs spoke to him directly, and he was insane.

"Do you talk to the bugs?" Rachel asked, trying not to reveal her nervousness.

"They talk to me sometimes. I can hear their voices in my head."

"And what have they told you?" Rachel glanced down at the redbug beneath her daughter's hand.

"They told me I need to listen to you. They told me I would be all grown up soon."

"You've grown fast," Rachel said. There was a twitch in her smile. "I want to take you east—to my family's house in Mirror Lake. Our family's house. Do you think you're well enough to leave now?"

"East," Carlotta said. She paused, as if she were listening for someone to comment on the word. Then she said, "Yes, east is a good direction."

Rachel watched as her daughter carefully lifted the two red-bugs from her body. She placed both on a nearby clump of egg sacs. The insects remained in their new positions. They appeared to be watching the mother and daughter.

Rachel took hold of Carlotta's hand. Rachel's wrist was now without pain. She pulled Carlotta toward the doorway, anxious to be away from the insects and egg sacs. "We're going to head down the beach to another house where Aunt Daphne and her girls are waiting for us. We won't be coming back to the pool house." She shivered when she pictured the three limp bodies that were dangling from the balcony.

"Goodbye," Carlotta whispered. Rachel realized she was speaking to the redbugs.

Rachel exhaled in relief when they reached the beach. She glanced in the direction of the mansion, but she could only see the silhouettes of the evergreens. She quickly led Carlotta across the rocks, and she was careful to avoid the two corpses. She didn't want her daughter to notice them.

She was grateful to be beside Carlotta, heading toward freedom. "We can take walks around Mirror Lake together," she said. "I used to do that with my parents when I was a young girl. We'd go for a swim at the end."

Carlotta smiled at her mother. "They told me I won't ever need to learn how to swim."

Startled by the comment, Rachel said, "But you could learn if you wanted to. You're your own person, Carlotta. You won't have to live by everything they tell you, just like you won't have to live by everything I tell you. You're going to make your own discoveries." She saw a look of terror seize her daughter's face.

"Mama! Behind you!"

Rachel was about to turn when she felt something hard smash into the back of her neck.

She dropped the lantern as she fell to the rocks. Pain bloomed in her neck and spread into her upper back. She rolled onto her side to look up at whoever had struck her.

The fallen lantern cast light on Nathaniel. He still wore his robe. Blood—most likely Rufus's—covered his chest and neck. He held a stone in one hand and a carving knife in the other. He stared down at Rachel with wild eyes.

"I've always known you were different from the rest of the girls, girls," he said.

Rachel looked around for Carlotta. She saw her daughter standing a few feet from her. She figured she could block Nathaniel's path to Carlotta. She slowly, achingly raised herself into a sitting position.

"You look like my real mother," Nathaniel continued. "My real mother who died, died."

"You've told me that before," Rachel said with irritation.

"But now I know that's not what makes you special. You don't just look like my mother, mother. I've received the message, message. You are my spiritual mother because you're going to witness my rising, rising, rising."

While Rachel stared into Nathaniel's eyes, she wrapped her hand around a fist-sized stone on the beach. If Nathaniel stepped any closer, she could stand and swing that stone into the side of his head.

"But you see there's a problem, problem we have to take care of before I rise."

"What's that?" Rachel asked, her grip on the stone tightening.

"The little monster, monster who's growing into a big monster." Nathaniel pointed the knife at Carlotta.

Rachel glanced at her daughter, who appeared to be mesmerized by Nathaniel. Rachel wondered how many times she'd spied on him through his bedroom window.

Rachel turned back to Nathaniel. "She's not a problem. She's going to walk down this beach and leave us alone. And then I'll be here so you can rise."

"But the monsters, monsters don't want me to rise," Nathaniel said. "They'll try to stop me. I'm not worried about Daphne's little monsters because they're still little. But this one's growing. She could act against me, me."

Rachel readied for her attack. She motioned for Nathaniel to come down to her level. She said in a soft voice, "I need to tell you something about that little monster."

Nathaniel dropped the stone and stepped toward her. He lowered himself to the ground, and that's when Rachel swung at him with her own stone.

Nathaniel caught her wrist and squeezed until she felt like it would break. The stone dropped with a thud.

"I received a message about you doing that, that," he said with a grin.

And then he slid the knife into one side of her stomach.

Rachel gasped.

"Mama!" Carlotta shrieked.

In shock, Rachel watched Nathaniel pull the blade out of her body. A circle of blood expanded on the front of her maid's uniform. She pressed her hand over the spot, but it continued to grow.

He smiled at her. "Don't worry, worry. You won't die yet. Not before I rise, rise. I received a message about that, too."

"Carlotta, run!" Rachel shouted.

"No more running." Nathaniel leapt over Rachel's body and grabbed Carlotta. Rachel saw them both tumble onto the beach.

"Don't hurt her!" she screamed.

The lantern's light showed Nathaniel raise his knife as Carlotta struggled to get out from underneath him. Rachel saw a large redbug land on his back. The bug scurried up to the base of his neck and thrust its abdomen toward his skin, puncturing flesh with its stinger.

Nathaniel's extended arm began to quiver. "No," he hissed. "They can't hurt me anymore, anymore."

Despite the hot, wet pain in her stomach, Rachel raised herself from the ground and stumbled toward Nathaniel and her daughter. The insect repeatedly moved its abdomen as if it were copulating with Nathaniel. A trickle of blood came from where the redbug's stinger entered him.

The knife fell to the beach.

Taking Carlotta's hand, Rachel helped her wiggle out from beneath Nathaniel. He tried to grab Carlotta, but he didn't seem to have control over his body. His limbs shook as the redbug continued its penetrating motion.

Nathaniel turned his head toward Rachel and her daughter. "I'll rise with the sun, sun," he said in a strained voice. "The living and the dead will see. My dad and stepmom will see. My dad and stepmom will-"

His eyes suddenly went blank and stared through Rachel.

"He's dead," she said with relief. She saw the redbug had inserted half its abdomen into Nathaniel's neck. The insect finally stopped moving and looked as if it were resting.

Rachel kept her hand over her wound as she embraced her daughter. "You're safe now, baby," she cooed.

"You're hurt, Mama. Stay here."

Rachel watched Carlotta run toward the redbug nests. She returned with her hands cupping the gelatinous egg sac substance. She gently applied the substance to her mother's wound, and Rachel felt that tingling sensation once again. She doubted the substance would keep her from bleeding to death, but at least it could keep her alive until she delivered Carlotta to Daphne.

"We need to keep moving," she said, fetching the lantern from the beach. "The house-"

An explosion interrupted her.

Rachel looked toward the mansion and saw the sky in the distance glowed pink. Another explosion sounded.

Bombs.

Rachel remembered the plane she'd heard tonight. She also recalled what Nathaniel had told her while she poured his orange juice one morning. "And if the government tries bombing us the way it did Spokane, it will find that we're immune. Our insect friends have made us immune."

The third explosion was louder and closer. Rachel could actually feel its heat. The evergreens bordering the beach were trembling.

"Mama!" Carlotta said.

Rachel saw her daughter point at Nathaniel, who was moving stiffly into a standing position. He still had the eyes of a corpse.

The redbug on his back fluttered its wings.

"It's them," Carlotta said with relief. "They're making him move."

Nathaniel motioned for Rachel and Carlotta to follow him. They walked toward the water, and Nathaniel pointed at the rowboat at the end of the pier. He remained near the beach while the mother and daughter headed toward the vessel.

Another explosion.

Rachel turned back toward the beach and saw flames rising in the sky past the mansion. "Hurry!" she told Carlotta. She grabbed her daughter's hand, and they ran the rest of the way to the rowboat. She helped Carlotta aboard and had her sit at the bow of the vessel. She set the lantern in the center of the boat and sat closer to the stern, with her back to her daughter. She untied the rope and rowed as quickly as possible.

Pain shot through her side, and she felt blood seeping through the substance covering her wound.

She kept rowing.

More explosions sounded, and the temperature continued to rise. Rachel gazed fearfully at the shore, which wasn't far enough away. Parts of the mansion's tiled roof were burning. All window curtains were aflame. The third-floor balcony from which Miyoko and the others had jumped was drooping. One of the palm trees by the pool house had become a ball of fire.

Rachel saw Nathaniel's body collapse on the beach.

She rowed more forcefully and tried to ignore the scorching air pressing against her face. She felt like her cheeks might melt and her hair would burn. She looked behind her and saw Carlotta was kneeling at the bow, one of her long arms trailing in the water.

Rachel remembered swimming in a shallow part of Mirror Lake one afternoon while Carlos accompanied her on an inner tube. He didn't know how to swim. Rachel floated past him, snickering at his fear of the water. He splashed her and joked, "If you stay in the lake too long our baby's going to turn into a tadpole."

Rachel noticed that Carlotta was now standing at the bow, facing the horizon. "That's not safe, baby," she said. "You're going to tip the boat."

Carlotta turned to look at her with a weirdly calm expression. She began removing her tank top, and another bomb burst.

Rachel watched the top floor of the mansion disintegrate in a yellow flash of light. She shut her eyes and shielded her face as the searing debris sprayed the boat. She then turned back toward Carlotta to make sure she hadn't been harmed.

Her daughter remained in a standing position. Long, translucent wings protruded from the skin of her bare back.

Wings Rachel had never seen before.

Wings that beat slowly at first and then fast enough to lift Carlotta over the water. The girl smiled down at her mother, her black eyes glinting from the fire on the shore.

ACKNOWLEDGEMENTS

I must first express gratitude to Montag Press. Thank you, Charlie Franco, for your enthusiasm about my novel and allowing *Red Swarm* to reach bookshelves both real and virtual. Nicholas Morine, I'm grateful you were willing to serve as editor for the book and help my prose hum more loudly. Thank you to my friends Kevin O'Brien, Bjorn Remmers, Josh Rogin, and Garth Stein for reading the entire manuscript and advising on what to keep and what to exterminate. Cheers to the members of my writers group—John Flick, Cate Goethals, Soyon Im, and, once again, Kevin and Garth. You offered invaluable feedback and suffered through many discussions about redbugs and neck wounds while eating pizza. Thank you to Stafford Lombard for continuously believing in me and inspiring me to write stories that aren't boring. I'm grateful to the Quorumites past and present who've been so supportive of my fiction. Jason Major, thanks for serving as my technical advisor. And finally, love and gratitude to my faithful family. Now you see how a minor bedbug phobia can turn into a novel about killer insects.